SVETI	SAINT
VITO	VITUS
PLEŠE	DANCES
ZA	ETERNITY
VJEČNOST	
sarajevska priča o duhovima	a sarajevo ghost story

Stewart von Allmen

Aida Mušanović

saint vitus dances eternity	*stewart von allmen*
book design and layout	*larry s. friedman*
art and bosnian translation	*aida mušanović*

St. Vitus Dances Eternity
Copyright ©1996 by Stewart von Allmen.

All rights reserved. This book may not be reproduced,
in whole or in part, without the written permission of the publisher, except for the purpose of reviews.

The characters and events described in this book are fictional. Any resemblance between the characters and any person, living or dead, is purely coincidental.

The mention of or reference to any companies or products in these pages is not a challenge to the trademarks or copyrights concerned.

Because of the mature themes presented within, reader discretion is advised.

White Wolf is committed to reducing waste in publishing. For this reason, we do not permit our covers to be "stripped" for returns, but instead require that the whole book be returned, allowing us to resell it.

Borealis is an imprint of White Wolf Publishing.

White Wolf Publishing | 780 Park North Boulevard | Suite 100 | Clarkston | Georgia | 30021

Dedicated to all
Bosnians — whether
Croat or Jew or Muslim
or Serb or whatever
their ethnicity — who
stood together for the
right to stay together.

For all people we wish such resistance to rhetoric and fear.

NESRETNA | UNHAPPY
JE | THE LAND THAT
ZEMLJA | HAS
KOJOJ |
SU | NEED OF
POTREBNI |
HEROJI. | HEROES.

Bertolt Brecht, Galilejev život —

— Bertolt Brecht, Life of Galileo

FOREWORD

A fragile but promising peace has begun to take hold in the Balkans. In Bosnia and Herzegovina, the country most devastated by the war, many thousands of families remain displaced and much of the infrastructure has been destroyed. The World Bank estimates that $5.1 billion will be needed in the first three years for basic reconstruction. Newspaper accounts combine stories of hope with continuing reports of conflict. Sarajevo, a symbol of both visible destruction and community courage, has begun repairs and its open-air markets are crowded with goods and with people. Yet the city and country are a long way from the relative prosperity of its pre-war days. Each family has water and gas only on certain hours of certain days, and there is a severe shortage of electricity. An urgent priority in Sarajevo and throughout Bosnia is to obtain enough resources to restart the economy, so that Bosnians may once again work for pay — not merely humanitarian aid packages — and earn their own living.

As Bosnia seeks to rebuild its public sector and encourage the growth of business and industry, critical human needs are being met not just by international organizations but also by an emerging nonprofit sector. During the war, citizens formed hundreds of voluntary organizations to help their communities. These groups, staffed mostly by volunteers, deliver an incredible range of services: they provide counseling to women and children displaced and traumatized by the war, offer extra educational support to such children, assist women who have been raped, get food and fuel to the elderly and handicapped, provide recreational activities for youth or encourage their interest in the arts, get glasses to the visually impaired, and provide services to children and adults disabled by the war. They work with young children through therapeutic puppet shows and with the elderly through handicrafts. They operate in collective centers, offices, schools, and private homes. Their leaders include psychiatrists, psychologists, teachers, nurses, social workers, homemakers, and retired people, many themselves displaced persons who have lost homes and family members in the war.

Some examples: Project Sanya, serving hundreds of women and children, is housed in a collective center in what used to be temporary quarters for railroad workers in Sarajevo. The director, a physicist who is herself a displaced person, gave birth to a daughter several months after her husband was killed while getting water for the family. Since she alone now supports her family, she must continue to work, and is a role model for so many other women. Project Selma, located in a private home in the old part of Sarajevo, provides educational services for children, some of whom have watched family members die and have forgotten how to play. Because space is limited, children come in shifts by age group. Ruhama, in Zenica, ensures that hundreds of elderly or disabled people receive food, fuel, and medical care, with the help of adult and teenaged volunteers. Red Lily, in Tuzla, provides volunteers to meet a wide range of community needs.

Formed to meet immediate, life-and-death needs, these organizations now plan to become ongoing nonprofit organizations. Such groups — known as NGOs: non-governmental organizations — are a major force for democracy and peace, offering citizens a way to participate in the rebuilding and renewal of Bosnian society. They can demonstrate democracy in action, and provide opportunities for multicultural cooperation.

Emerging NGOs face great challenges, especially in a country devastated by war and with no history of an independent nonprofit sector. Groups must learn how to structure themselves, establish a governance structure, plan and implement projects, develop relationships with other organizations and with government ministries and effectively use volunteers — all the while carrying out the dozens of other activities expected of a nonprofit organization. Unlike NGOs in the United States, they must do all this without role models and with almost no Bosnian-language manuals or other literature available to help them.

Some Bosnian NGOs have received initial funding from relief organizations, United Nations bodies, foreign governments, individuals, and a very few foundations. International organizations are also beginning to provide organizational development assistance, helping groups establish governing structures, plan programs, and raise funds. However, the emphasis is on bringing international consultants to assist the groups, rather than on developing local capacity to support the independent sector.

The New Bosnia Fund (NBF) was established to fill that gap. A nonprofit, nonpartisan, nonpolitical organization established in the U.S. and in Bosnia in 1995, NBF exists to support the nonprofit sector, thus promoting democracy, pluralism, and tolerance in Bosnia and Herzegovina. NBF is committed to developing Bosnian capacity to nurture its own nonprofit sector through working cooperatively with organizations and individuals throughout the world. NBF priorities include the following:

- To provide support for nonprofit, nonpartisan, nonpolitical organizations inside and outside Bosnia that foster the renewal and development of Bosnia and Herzegovina as a multicultural and democratic community and assist Bosnian refugees and displaced persons.
- To encourage public support of the nonprofit sector by all segments of Bosnian society — government, the private sector, and the general pubic.
- To provide public education in Bosnia, the United States, and other countries to provide an understanding of the needs of the Bosnian community and of Bosnian nonprofit organizations, and to encourage people to provide assistance including voluntary services.

...

NBF's leadership includes two young physicians from Sarajevo, an advisor at the Bosnian embassy in Washington, D.C., and the Presidents of two nonprofit organizations in the U.S. which have provided organizational development assistance to emerging Bosnian NGOs: MOSAICA and Refugee Women in Development. Additionally, MOSAICA provided a six-week internship in the United States for the two physicians, so they could spend time with U.S. nonprofit organizations and see several models for providing capacity-building assistance to such groups.

In Bosnia, NBF has the support of a multicultural group of respected professionals. With a grant from the Miranda Foundation, NBF has begun to develop its organizational infrastructure and link NGOs with potential funders and other sources of assistance. NBF identified five Sarajevo-based organizations serving children and youth to receive the proceeds of a special event organized by the Fund for the Future of Our Children that raised over $20,000. NBF is now in contact with more than 60 NGOs in the Sarajevo, Zenica, and Tuzla regions, as well as with many nonprofit organizations and funders outside the country. Building on these contacts, NBF is working to develop a network linking Bosnian organizations with each other and with similar organizations in other countries. NBF is also working to establish a library of materials developed for nonprofit organizations, modified to fit the needs of Bosnian NGOs, and translated into Bosnian. It plans to offer training and individual consultation to NGOs.

Most important, NBF — with the help of MOSAICA and other organizations — will work to develop a group of Bosnians who are trained to assist NGOs. In the future, when most international relief organizations have left Bosnia, NBF will remain as an ongoing, locally controlled source of support for the nation's independent sector.

...

The proceeds from the sale of this story will help support the work of the New Bosnia Fund. Tax-exempt contributions to the organization can be made in the United States to:

**MOSAICA:
The Center for Nonprofit Development and Pluralism**

1000 16th Street, N.W., Suite 604
Washington, D.C. 20036

Telephone: (202) 887-0620.

Identify that your donation is intended for the New Bosnia Fund.

Centurion Gustičić, a stern but likable man, stood several feet away and watched carefully for interlopers, his eyes casually flicking over the scrambling people, while I and the five other Legionnaires who formed the patrol tried to extricate the dead, the newcomers to our world.

Saint Vitus Dances Eternity: a sarajevo ghost story
Sveti Vito Pleše za Vječnost: sarajevska priča o duhovima

I've always felt I existed between two worlds.

3

Raščišćavanje je sporo napredovalo. Ulica Vase Miskina i obližnja tržnica bile su smrvljene. Granatna paljba sa okolnih brda pretvorila je u prah ovu prometnu pješačku zonu. Sjenke su ovdje bile vrlo guste - a granica koja me je razdvajala od mog predjašnjeg svijeta tanušna - tako da ono, što mi se učinilo da je krš ruševina, zapravo su bile ruke, noge i glave preko kojih sam puzio da bih se odmakao od usplahirenih i zbunjenih Sarajlija. Centurion Gustičić, ozbiljan ali prijazan muškarac, stajao je udaljen nekoliko koraka pažljivo vrebajući na uljeze. Njegov pogled je neodredjeno treperio po gomili ljudi koji su se gurali, dok smo ja, i pet drugih Legionara što su činili patrolu, pokušavali da izvučemo mrtve, novopridošlice u naš svijet.

Stao sam pored jedne od *nastradalih*. Poveća betonska gromada, što je bio vjerovatno komad ceste izbijen bljuvanjem granatne paljbe iz minobacača, ležala je preko nogu žene kojoj sam prišao.

Naredba Centuriona Gustičića bila je kratka: "Požuri, ima i drugih."

Tačno. Eksplozija je bila strašna. Mrtvi su bili posvuda.

"Možda će preživjeti," rekoh, ali čučnuvši pored nje odmah sam vidio da nisam bio u pravu - grudni koš joj je počeo tamniti bojeći njenu svijetlu kožu dok joj je srce ispumpavalo krv ne samo iz rupe od gelera na grudima nego i u njen torzo takodje, natapajući pluća, jetru i ostale organe. Žudio sam da zaustavim *krvarenje*, da joj otvorim grudni koš i stegnem arteriju kroz koju je oticao njen život; i iako sam u životu bio hirurg, nisam mogao ništa da učinim. Sada moj posao nije započinjao sve dok pacijent ne bude mrtav.

Posmatrao sam je izbliza, njen život je poput violinske žice što titra po tonu i gubi ton. Oči joj se otvoriše i bljesnuše, i mislim da me je bar za trenutak morala ugledati. Ali i da je pored sebe zatekla živog čovjeka, ne bi reagovala drugačije. Žena u nekom drugom gradu koji nije razoren ratom bi mogla posumnjati u ono što vidi, ali otkrio sam prije nešto više od mjesec dana, da duhovima naseljeno područje Sarajeva, što mi je sada vidljivo, nije ništa sumornije od realnosti na ulicama.

The clean-up progressed slowly. Vaso Miskin Street and the adjoining market area were pulped. Shellfire from the surrounding hills had pulverized the busy pedestrian area. The shadows were so thick here — and the barrier that divided me from my previous world so thin — that I mistook for rubble the arms and legs and heads I crawled over to stay clear of the frantic and confused Sarajevans. Centurion Gustičić, a stern but likable man, stood several feet away and watched carefully for interlopers, his eyes casually flicking over the scrambling people, while I and the five other Legionnaires who formed the patrol tried to extricate the dead, the newcomers to our world.

I stood over one *victim*. A large boulder of concrete, probably a portion of the street disgorged in the vomit of fire induced by the mortar shell, lay across the legs of the woman I tended.

Centurion Gustičić's command was terse: "Hurry, there are others."

It was true. The blast had been terrible. The dead were everywhere.

"She might live," I said, but squatting at her side I saw immediately that I was wrong — her chest was turning dark, pigmenting her fair skin as her heart pumped blood not only out the shrapnel hole in her chest but into her torso as well, where it lubricated her lungs and liver and everything else. I yearned to staunch the *blood*, to cut her open and compress the artery leaking her life away; though in life I'd been a surgeon, I could do nothing. Now my work didn't begin until my patient was dead.

I watched her closely, her life a violin string oscillating on key and off. Her eyes flickered open, and for a moment I think she must have seen me. But she didn't react differently than if she'd found a living man by her side. A woman in a city not torn apart by war might have questioned what she saw, but as I'd discovered little more than a month ago, the ghost-haunted terrain of Sarajevo visible to me now is no darker than the reality of the streets.

I was an agnostic at the nexus of Catholicism, Orthodoxy, Islam and Judaism.

I've always felt I existed between two worlds. Every facet of my life personified dichotomy. Certainly as an ethnic Serb I defied easy classification, caught as I was in a city in a nation that was itself once caught on the crossroads of great empires. The Hapsburgs and the Ottomans made sport of this land for centuries. I was drawn, ultimately drawn apart, by patriotism and nationalism, which is essentially the difference of pride in my country and making others proud of my country. Divided between a supposed ethnic ancestry and a lifelong devotion to my heartland home of Sarajevo. But there was more. I was a pacifist caught between generations of more serious-minded males: my father the Četnik Serb and my anti-Serb son. I was an agnostic at the nexus of Catholicism, Orthodoxy, Islam and Judaism. Even in my job as a surgeon, I daily walked that dreadful, teetering axis that is life and *death*. And now, my prior life as a doctor offering but a crude glimpse of this damned world, I was suspended in this purgatory between life and nonexistence.

It's a purgatory where the dichotomy of existence is very different than the struggle between life and death waged by the living around me now — a dizzying whirl of panic and flight that left me as lost in the crowd as I was in my thoughts.

All the baggage from life that implores us to concern ourselves with body and spirit is reduced to simple concern for spirit here. Perhaps finally in death, humankind can escape the pummeling roll of the wheel of history, of fortune, for we become disengaged enough to actually concern ourselves with the state of the future, a development only allowed when apprehension for physical health is eliminated.

My name is Dragoš Miloslavić, and you already know more about me than I could recall for the first days that I wandered the *haunted* streets of Sarajevo.

As soon as I recognized my ghostly state and tore down layers of denial to acknowledge my appalling situation (imagine a doctor surrounded not by the dying but by the already dead!), I immediately dropped the appellative "doctor." It made no sense here, and only subjected me to additional scrutiny by those who did not know I was firmly entrenched in the Hierarchy, the pointed and pointless way the dead name the main bloc here.

It's a purgatory where the dichotomy of existence is very different than the struggle between life and death waged by the living around me now —
a dizzying whirl of panic and flight that left me as lost in the crowd as I was in my thoughts.

Iz nekog razloga, svi su pretpostavljali da sam pripadao toj prezira zaslužnoj grupi plaćenih lešinara zvanih "Žeteoci smrti." Očigledno da reputacija doktora nepravedno trpi čak i u zemlji mrtvih, iako je tačno da mnogi doktori postanu Žeteoci smrti; isto tako kao što postoje doktorati onih koji su još uvijek medju živima i koji su požnjeli život iz mog grada. Žeteoci su fanatici smrti koji lebde nad umirućim očekujući posljednji izdah u nadi da će novi mrtvac, kojega ponekad nazivamo "Infant" ili "Dijete" stići ovdje kao duh. Inače, oni će transcendirati - prekoračiti do onoga što nas očekuje bilo da je to raj, a, vjerovatnije je, samo još jedan *mizerni* pakao sa novim pravilima za prokletstvo, razočarenje i izolaciju - ili će potpuno iščeznuti u Zaborav, mračnu prazninu za što sam u životu očekivao da je smrt, i čije se odsutnosti sada najviše bojim i nalazim je neshvatljivom.

Zli duhovi, čiji je jedini cilj da ulove novu dušu i okoriste se time, mogu lako da prevare Dijete, dok su mu vid i razboritost još u pometnji, ovijeni plazmičnom košuljicom koju sve pridošlice nose kao drugu embrionsku vrećicu. Žeteoci su neka vrsta lovaca na plijen u zagrobnom životu i za njih riječi "mrtav ili živ" nemaju nikakvoga značenja.

Duše mrtvih imaju vrijednost, jer su one, ironijom sudbine, jedino što udiše novi život u ove predjele naseljene bićima - ljudima? - toliko drevnim da se kaže da više nisu prepoznatljivi kao nešto što je jednom bilo ljudsko. A možda nikada i nisu bili ljudi. Ja znam tako malo o ovom novom svijetu... ali doista znam da Djeca koju "spašavaju" Žeteoci neminovno završe u okovima, dok oni kojih oslobode hijerarhijske patrole kao što je moja, idu u Stygiju, daleki dom onih što vladaju Hijerarhijom. U gradu, pretpostavljam, postoji potreba da se život ponovo otkrije i da se uživa u njegovim brojnim prijatnim običajima i nježnim radostima. Spašene duše nalaze utjehu u gradu smrti i čine ga lijepim, a Gospodari smrti i duhovi davno umrlih koji već naseljavaju grad, bivaju stalno obnovljeni dušama koje, iako nisu žive, barem su kraće mrtve. Priznajem, neki Žeteoci sakupljaju Duše koje će poslati u Stygiju, i to za odredjenu cijenu; *iskorištavati* na ovakav način, za ličnu dobit, očito je grijeh, ukoliko jedan agnostik smije da osudjuje.

Veliki točak se i dalje okreće - ljudska priroda postoji i poslije groba, što su strašne vijesti za one koji su još uvijek živi i možda se nadaju odmoru od sitničavih poslodavaca što im zadaju brige i idiota koji ih obasipaju uvredama. I ovo svakako nije dobrodošlica za one koji su već prepatili kroz pakao u životu, kao što su oni u mom izmučenom domu pod opsadom u Sarajevu, u Bosni.

For some reason everyone assumed I belonged to that despicable class of mercenary vultures called "reapers." The reputation of doctors apparently suffers unfairly even in the land of the dead, though it's true that many doctors become reapers, just as some doctorates still among the living have reaped life from my city. Reapers are the zealots of death that hover over the dying in anticipation of that last gasp with a hope that the newly dead, who we sometimes refer to as an Enfant, will arrive here as a ghost. Otherwise, they will transcend — pass to whatever awaits us, be it heaven or, far more likely, just another *miserable* hell with new rules for damnation and frustration and isolation — or fade completely into Oblivion, the dark void that in life is what I expected death to be, but which is the absence I now fear most and find incomprehensible.

The Enfant, his or her vision and wits bound into confusion by a plasmic caul which all who arrive wear like a second embryonic sac, is easily tricked by these fiends whose only aim is to gather the new soul and profit by it. They're like afterlife bounty hunters, although for reapers "dead or alive" holds no meaning.

The souls of the dead have value, for ironically they are all that breathe new life into these lands inhabited by beings — people? — so ancient they are said to be no longer recognizable as something once human. Perhaps they were never human. I know so little of this new world... but I do know that Enfants "rescued" by reapers inevitably end up in chains, while those liberated by Hierarchy patrols such as mine go to Stygia, the far-away home of those who govern the Hierarchy. In the city, there is a need, I suppose, to discover life again and savor its many delicate forms and fragile delights. The saved souls find solace in a city of death they make beautiful, and the Deathlords and the spirits of the long-dead already inhabiting the city are constantly renewed by those who, if not alive, are at least less dead than they. Admittedly, some reapers gather souls they will send to Stygia, but for a price, and to *exploit* in this way for personal gain is clearly a sin, if an agnostic can cast such stones.

But that great wheel spins ever on — human nature does exist beyond the grave, which is dire news for those who still live and may hope for respite from the petty masters who pain them and the idiots who lavish them with indignities. And this is certainly not welcome news for those who have already suffered through hell in life, such as those in my beleaguered and battered home of Sarajevo, Bosnia.

Reapers are the zealots of death that hover over the dying in anticipation of that last gasp with a hope that the newly dead... will arrive here as a ghost.

I to je zašto smo moje kolege Legionari i ja posvećeni multikulturnom, mulitreligioznom - i zaboga multiljudskom! - bivstvovanju što Sarajevo utjelovljava! Svi smo mi žrtve ovog nacionalističkog napada na Bosnu koji nije izazvan. Odlučili smo da ostanemo ovdje umjesto da pobjegnemo i predahnemo u Stygiji. I svi smo poginuli u Sarajevu, sa izuzetkom Mehmeda, Muslimana, kojeg su srpske terorističke udarne snage ubile u Bijeljini, gradu u sjeveroistocnoj Bosni gdje je on posjećivao rodbinu.

I dok svijet općenito gleda na ovaj rat kao na dokaz neuspjeha onoga što je Bosna nastojala da predstavlja, u stvarnosti je zapravo sasvim suprotno. Sarajevo, uistinu, čak i sada, stoji kao putokaz na putanji ljudske istorije. Jer čak i nakon skoro dva mjeseca granatiranja i snajperskih napada koji su *desetkovali* stanovništvo smrću i prinudnim odlascima, Srbi i Hrvati i Muslimani i Jevreji još uvijek zajedno rade i preživljavaju. I svi oni odbijaju da odu, kao što sam i ja odbio dok sam bio živ, jer vjeruju u ono što ovaj grad predstavlja. Bez obzira na to što se svijet van Balkana pravi da ne vidi ovaj "konflikt," ovaj rat, baveći se svojim vlastitim sitnim problemima, terorističkim prijetnjama ili privredama koje opadaju.

Bez obzira na to što je znak koji upućuje na bolju budućnost sada izgubljen, dok nas ostatak svijeta zaobilazi na svom putu ka vlastitom Zaboravu.

Čak i ako se ostatak svijeta ne pomjeri da zaštiti nevine koji žive u gradu, Sarajlije mogu, barem u smrti, naći pojačanje. Legionari Hijerarhije su tu, na dohvat ruke, da se pobrinu za njih! Za razliku od neefikasnih Plavih šljemova Zaštitnih snaga Ujedinjenih Nacija, mi zaista intervenišemo, i odista smo dirnuti ovom *tragedijom* i ne tražimo da se njome okoristimo. Mi smo Plavi šljemovi zemlje mrtvih.

Ali vidjevši smrt na licu ove žene, prije nego što joj tijelo shvati da se bliži kraj, zapitah se kako možemo spasiti i žive i umiruće. Možemo li zamijeniti neefikasne Zastitne snage Ujedinjenih Nacija i u zemlji živih? Odbijam da prepatim još jedan Vukovar, što je UNPROFOR dopustio. Taj hrvatski grad je pao u ruke Srbima nakon tromjesečne opsade, krajem prošle godine, a ljudi Vukovara su pretrpili dane pokolja po ulicama dok su Srbi uplesali u grad i slavili pobjedu.

Možda zbog toga što sam već mrtav, pa mogu surovo da predvidjam smrt. Poput letimičnog pogleda na ulupinu u automobilu, prije nego što se saobraćajna nesreća zaista desi, tako i ja mogu da vidim smrt na licima, na tijelima onih čiji se kraj približava. Baš kao što to vidim i na licu ove žene, mogu da pregledam gomilu ljudi i jasno vidim da se ovaj užas neće skoro završiti.

And that's why my fellow Legionnaires and I are all dedicated to the multi-cultural, multi-religious — the by-god-multi-human! — existence that Sarajevo embodied! All of us are victims of this unprovoked nationalistic assault on Bosnia. We decided to remain instead of flee to reprieve in Stygia. And except for Mehmed, a Muslim who was killed by a terrorist-led Serbian strike force in the northeastern Bosnia town of Bijeljina where he was visiting relatives, we were all killed inside Sarajevo.

While the world at large may see this war as evidence of the failure of what Bosnia sought to represent, it's really quite the opposite. Indeed, Sarajevo stands like a road sign on the roadway of human history even now. For even after almost two months of shelling and sniper attacks that have *decimated* the population by the death and the departures they have forced, Serbs and Croats and Muslims and Jews still work and survive side by side. And they all refuse to leave, as I refused while I still lived, because they believe in what this city represents. So no matter that the world outside the Balkans may turn a dry, blind eye to this "conflict," this war, as they deal with their own small problems, their terrorist threats or sagging economies.

No matter that a sign marking a better future is now lost as the rest of the world detours us on their way to their own Oblivion.

Even if the rest of the world will not move to protect the innocents who live in the city, at least in death Sarajevans can find succor. The Legionnaires of the Hierarchy are at hand to tend them! Unlike the ineffective Blue Helmets of the United Nations Protection Force, we actually intervene, we are actually moved by this *tragedy* and do not seek to profit by it. We are the Blue Helmets of the lands of the dead.

But seeing death on this woman's face before her body realizes the end is near makes me wonder how we can save both the living and the dying. Can we replace the impotent United Nations Protection Force in the lands of the living too? I refuse to endure another Vukovar, which UNPROFOR allowed. That Croatian city fell to the Serbs after a three-month siege at the end of last year, and the people of Vukovar endured days of slaughter in the streets as the Serbs danced into the city and celebrated their victory.

Perhaps because I'm dead already, I have a cruel foresight of death. Like glimpsing a dent in an automobile before an accident actually occurs, so too can I see death in the faces, on the bodies, of those approaching their time. Just as I see it in the face of this woman, I can inspect the crowd and I can plainly see that this horror will not soon end.

Saint Vitus Dances Eternity

The Enfant, his or her vision and wits bound into confusion by a plasmic caul which all who arrive wear like a second embryonic sac, is easily tricked by these fiends whose only aim is to gather the new soul and profit by it.

A little girl crying at the feet of her dead mother seems to have skin pulled back to reveal a *skull* spider-webbed with fractures.

An old man with an expressionless face and a small hole over his breast that weeps a slow red drip.

A family huddled together in a corner counts their numbers and their blessings. All have withered, crispy skin, except the oldest daughter will live because she won't be with her loved ones when they burn.

Couldn't I follow these doomed souls and protect them from the reapers and salvage their essences for perpetual protection in Stygia? Alas, anywhere but in Sarajevo, where the soon-to-die outnumber not just the dead but seem more prominent too than the living. But at the current rate of death forecast over a period of a couple years — though it's ridiculous to think that even this inattentive, *irrational* world will suffer the hateful, warmongering fools Milošević and Karadžić to live even half that long, or even until the end of 1992 — the dead will outnumber the living. The ghosts of the afterlife will become the guardian angels of the damned. Where else but in Sarajevo would such divine sentinels be ghosts, not angels?

Is this the sign of a city torn by ethnic strife? Where even after death we all fight for the other?

"Dragoš!" The Centurion's call brought me back.

The woman was dead.

"Yes, sir," I hastily acknowledged, amazing myself that conforming to a hierarchy of command was coming so easily for one always so independent in life. But order was naturally at the heart of the Hierarchy. It allowed all their efforts to run as smoothly as this one in Sarajevo, I suppose.

As I watched, the woman seemed to swim across the barrier between our worlds. She wavered, drawn perhaps toward transcendence or possibly to Oblivion, but like so many in this city she was still tied to the life she so recently (and abruptly) departed; thus she became a ghost like myself.

For even after almost two months of shelling and sniper attacks that have decimated the population by the death and the departures they have forced, Serbs and Croats and Muslims and Jews still work and survive side by side.

Poput maske za ronjenje, da zaštiti tokom plivanja kroz neizmjerne dubine i nepoznate zadatke, plazmična košuljica je štitila ženu od još uvijek vidljivog užasa masakra u Ulici Vase Miskina. Štogod da je žena sada vidjela kasnije će joj se činiti samo kao san. Za trenutak sam se prisjetio jezivih stvari što sam sanjao dok sam lutao u svojoj plazmičnoj košuljici prije no što me našao Legionar Gustičić. Još gora je bila dezorijentacija i *tuga*, naročito kada se košuljica podigne po prvi put. Ali ipak, odahnuo sam znajući da će žena zasada biti pošteđena bola zbog Gustičićeve naredbe da se ostavi omotana u košuljicu.

Soptala je i bacakala se, ali sam je ja zgrabio i uspio dovući do Gustičića. Dvoje drugih je već bilo privezano za njega svilenim užetom što je on koristio u ovakvim prilikama. Na početku je imao samo zardjale okove, ali kako je organizacija u Hijerarhiji u gradu postajala bolja, postale su dostupne i bolje zalihe.

Izbavio sam desetak ovakve Djece na isti način, pa ipak me je obeshrabrivalo to da ženu ostavim samu. Bila je bijele rase, možda Srpkinja po nacionalnosti kao i ja, uhvaćena u požaru nacionalizma što je postavljao zahtjev u moje ime da se želim osloboditi Bosne i pridružiti Velikoj Srbiji. Kao Persefona koja je ostavila cvijeće da raste u tragovima njenih koraka po povratku iz Hada, tako i je Srbin napuštao srpsko tlo. Barem je to ono što tvrdi Milošević, gdje jedan Srbin kroči - to je Srbija.

Žena je drhturila, ali bili su tu i ostali koji su više patili, pa sam se ponovo okrenuo prema sceni katastrofe i tražio druge spremne da pobjegnu iz sarajevskog pakla u ono za što su očekivali da budu utješne ruke smrti.

Posmatrajući zemlju što se rasprsla i hipnotizirane i izranjavane ljude, pokušao sam da zamislim trg u ulici Vase Miskina kako to vide oči nekog živog Sarajlije. Premda je to bilo teško, jer je moj novi teren odražavao Sarajevo, ali je nudio iskrivljen pregled. Tako sam mogao zamisliti dim, što je štipao njihove oči, i suze. Prašina što je nadolazila u talasima i zadržavala se u naborima i otvorima njihove odjeće, kao i u njihovim ušima, nosevima i ustima. Zar usijanih *plamenova* što su uništavali ovdje neka prevrnuta teretna kola a tamo topili kožu sredovječnog čovjeka čija je duša transcendirala. Ali, ja sam bio odvojen od neposrednosti osjećaja. Oh, znao sam kakav je užas i zločin što osjećaju ovi smrtni svjedoci. I mogao sam to bolje analizirati.

Like a diving mask to protect her during that swim through unfathomable depths and unknowable tests, the woman's caul protected her against the still visible horror of the Vaso Miskin Street massacre. What she saw now would seem only dreams to her later. For an instant I recollected the awful things I dreamt as I wandered in my caul before Legionnaire Gustičić found me. Worse was the disorientation and *grief* — especially the grief — when the caul was first lifted. But still I sighed in relief, knowing Gustičić's order to leave the Enfants cauled would spare this woman for now.

She was gasping and thrashing, but I grabbed her and managed to haul her to Gustičić. There were already two others attached to him by the silken cord he used in such instances. All he'd had at first were rusted manacles, but as the organization of the Hierarchy in the city became better, more appropriate supplies became available.

Though I'd delivered a dozen such Enfants this way, it was still unnerving to leave the woman's side. She was Caucasian, perhaps another ethnic Serb like me caught in the fire of the nationalists who made the claim in my name that I wanted to be free of Bosnia to join them in a greater Serbian state. But like Persephone who left flowers trailing in her footsteps after her return from Hades, so an ethnic Serb left Serbian soil. At least according to Milošević, who claimed that where a Serb walked, there was Serbia.

The woman was trembling, but there were others suffering more, so I turned to face the catastrophic scene again and to look for another ready to flee the hell of Sarajevo to what they expected to be the comforting arms of death.

Looking at the ruptured earth and the mesmerized and stricken people, I tried to imagine the marketplace of Vaso Miskin Street with the eyes of a living Sarajevan. It was difficult though, because my new terrain mirrored Sarajevo, but it offered a skewed view. So I could imagine the smoke, along with tears, that burned their eyes; dust that billowed and sought hold in the folds and gaps in their clothing, as well as in their ears, noses and mouths. The heat of the scattered *flames*, here razing an overturned produce cart, there melting the skin of a middle-aged man whose soul transcended. But I was distanced from the immediacy of emotion. Oh, I knew the terror and outrage these mortal witnesses felt. But I could dissect it better.

Saint Vitus Dances Eternity

But seeing death on this woman's face before her body realizes the end is near makes me wonder how we can save both the living and the dying.

Stojeći iza njih imao sam takodje i pogled odozgo. Jezive, besmislene šeme što su vladale ljudima postajale su jasnije sa moje tačke gledišta. Moja perspektiva je postajala sve nepristrasnija kako sam tražio da obavljam humane zadatke u Hijerarhiji, i nadgledao tek umrle kako se bore zahtijevajući vječnost. I nisam zaboravljao da je taj humani zadatak bio za ove ljude, moje kolege u životu.

Bila je to *groteskna* pozicija prednosti i to takva koja je i grotesko lijepa. Ovdje je vladala duboka tišina. Neka vrsta muka punog strahopoštovanja kao u džamiji. I ako se svijet činio udaljenijim i manje neposrednim, to je bilo zato što su boje bile tamnije. Mrtvije. Kao da je naslaga kredne prašine bila raspršena da sve priguši. Ili, kao da vidim svijet, iznenada sam shvatio, kroz purpurnu sliku čovjeka koji kleči u plaštu, kakav sam i ja nakratko imao kao dijete.

Moje misli su ponovo odlutale, hitnost Centurionovih naredbi je blijedila dok sam postajao onesposobljen kao i Sarajlije na trgu i dozvoljavao da me hipnotiše čudna ljepota pejsaža. Bio sam dijete okružen nebeskom tišinom u nekoj pravoslavnoj crkvi i zurio sam u životnu vrevu kroz veliki vitražni prozor koji je dominirao jednim od zidova. Sjećam se kako sam istezao vrat da bih mogao gledati svijet kroz različito obojena okna. Žuta što je činila radnička lica kao da su oboljeli od žutice. Crvena što je ljudske obraze činila poput sazrelih plodova i pridodavala zgradama auru nepobjedivosti. Zelena što je davala nestvarnu čistoću lišću u nepreglednim redovima stabala što su nekad zasadjena na ulicama. I purpurna sa plašta čovjeka koji kleči. Taj čovjek je bio sagnut u smjernoj molitivi drugome. Možda je darivao poklon. Ne sjećam se. Slika u prozoru nije bila toliko važna, nego to što je mijenjala moju predstavu realnog života napolju.

Tako prelijepa boja, ta purpurna. Postavio sam bezbroj zahtjeva svome ocu da sjedi mirno, dok sam se ja pomicao tamo-amo da bih stvorio liniju prizora sa čovjekom koji kleči i nekim predmetom izvana. Ono što sam konačno vidio bio je letimičan pogled na Sarajevo, kao što ga duh vidi sada. Svijet je izgledao *uvenulo*. Zelene i crvene su postale smedje. Kao i svaka druga treperava boja koju sam mogao opaziti. Boja lica ljudi, doduše, zadobila je raskoš nijanse što je nadjačavala sveopštu sivost i ispjeganost njihove kože. Izgledalo je da dostižu dubinu što običan pogled nije mogao otkriti. Ovo je, takodje, bilo slično tome kako živi sada izgledaju meni. Iako su bili na ivici smrti, posjedovali su čvrstu, grubu vezu sa svijetom, veze što duhovi kao ja posjeduju veoma rijetko.

My view from beyond them also allotted sight from above them. The terrible, petty designs that ruled men became clearer from my vantage. My perspective was becoming more clinical as I sought to do the humane tasks of the Hierarchy and overlook the merely dead to struggle to claim the undying. But I could not forget that the humane task was for these humans, my comrades in life.

It was a *grotesque* vantage, but one that was grotesquely beautiful. There was a stillness here. The kind of reverential silence that takes hold in a mosque. And if the world seemed more distant, less immediate, then it was because its color was greyer. Deader. As if a layer of chalk dust was spread to mute it. Or, as if, I realized suddenly, I saw the world through the purple lens of a kneeling man's robe, as I had briefly as a child.

My mind wandered again, the urgency of the Centurion's commands fading as I became as incapable as the Sarajevans in the marketplace and allowed the strange beauty of the landscape to mesmerize me. I was a child surrounded by heavenly silence in an Orthodox church, and I gazed at the bustle of life through the large stained-glass window that dominated one of the walls. I remember craning my neck so I could look at the world through the different colored panes. Yellow that jaundiced the working faces. Red that ripened people's cheeks and lent an aura of invincibility to the buildings. Green that gave an unreal clarity to the leaves of the unending rows of trees that once lined the streets. And the purple of the kneeling man's robe. The man was bent in supplication to another. Perhaps presenting a gift. I don't remember. The picture in the window wasn't as important as how it changed my image of the real world outside.

Such a beautiful color, purple. I'd drawn more than one demand from my father to sit still as I wriggled by his side to create a line of sight with the kneeling man and an object outside. What I eventually saw was a glimpse of Sarajevo as a ghost sees it now. The world looked *wilted*. Greens and reds became browns. As did every vibrant color I could spot. The complexion of the people outside, though, acquired a richness of hue that overcame the general graying and mottling of their skin. They seemed to achieve a depth that ordinary vision couldn't detect. That too was similar to how the living seemed to me now. Although they might be on the verge of death, they possessed a gripping and raw connection to the world, connections that ghosts such as I possess only tenuously.

Saint Vitus Dances Eternity

As I watched, the woman seemed to swim across the barrier between our worlds.

So, as through the lens of that kneeling man, I witnessed the carnage of the marketplace again. Around the perimeter of the damaged area stood countless Sarajevans hypnotized by the brutal *reality* of the destruction before them. In the unlikely event this war goes on for long, these same people, the ones not part of the pile of corpses themselves, will react more efficiently. Maybe save more lives. Now, only those with the proper training are able to react. The implausibility, the seeming impossibility, of bombs dropping on children in the midst of their city is beyond their comprehension.

It's almost too much for me. But stained-glass and death: grotesque beauty. That's my world now.

We worked for another five minutes before the first reaper showed himself. He was a tricky one, but his was a game the Centurion had warned us about. I would never have noticed otherwise. He was possessing a man... skinriding him to death. I noticed him only because I'd so carefully examined the crowd a few moments before. If Centurion Gustičić later disciplined me for slothfulness and risking the souls of the Sarajevans, I would have this as my defense.

The reaper was rapidly growing insubstantial as he slipped his gossamer form into his prey, but I saw him well enough to note that he wore some sort of insignia. I couldn't make it out, but I was more concerned with the reaper himself. His features darkened as he completed the maneuver. He was a middle-aged man and had perhaps been fifty when he died. The skillful deftness he displayed in his maneuver made me assume he'd been dead longer than the few months of this war.

The man the reaper was skinriding was one in whose face I'd read great horror. Moments before he had been frantically wiping his arm as if the sprayed drops were acid, not blood. Or if fearful like Lady Macbeth that the invisible spots were indelible and marked him forever as part of this *madness*. He certainly wasn't the kind that would ever harden to such tragedies. So when I saw him assisting the wounded, I paused again, just long enough to note that the person he was assisting was beyond help. He wasn't quite dead either, but almost. I could see through the mirror of the man's blank eyes that his brain had been severely bruised and death was imminent.

For an instant I recollected the awful things I dreamt as I wandered in my caul before Legionnaire Gustičić found me.

Da je Žeteoc mogao odnijeti umirućeg čovjeka na neko mjesto daleko od ove pustoši, možda iza ili u središte gomile, gdje ni ja niti drugi Legionari ga ne bi vidjeli, mogao bi se kradomice udaljiti sa dušom Djeteta kao nagradom. Nisam mogao opaziti nikakav znak da bi ovaj čovjek mogao nanovo hodati poslije smrti, ali ponašao sam se pod pretpostavkom da je Žeteoc znao bolje.

Žeteoc je počinjao brže se kretati. Zaostali *grčevi* života su protresli čovjeka koji je sada bio mrtav. Osigurao sam da najmanje jedan od drugara pažljivo motri na moj poduhvat, prije no što sam se usudio da podjem u potragu za Žeteocem. Izbjegavao sam gužvu što sam više mogao, ali čak i tako, nekoliko Sarajlija je nabasalo na mene i stvaralo neugodnosti dok sam se ja žurio prema leševima. Ali svjetina je prodrmala i Žeteoca, i on je, zajedno sa svojim teretom, bio gurnut na zemlju. Jedno Dijete je već počelo izranjati iz leša.

Žeteoc je bio van moga domašaja, jer je posjedovao u vlasti živoga čovjeka čime je i on sam postajao dio živoga kraljevstva. Mogao sam pokušati da naštetim smrtniku kojeg je on držao u vlasti ali odbio sam tu mogućnost, pošto sam se trudio da zaštitim Sarajlije. Pa čak i tako, bila je to pat pozicija. I ja sam bio izvan njegovoga domašaja, takodje. Srećom, Dijete je pristizalo na moju stranu plašta.

Žeteoc je, vjerujem, bio spreman da se bori za svoj teret, ali moja kolegica Legionarka, Pava Šačić, Hrvatica po nacionalnosti, jedna od prvih koji su ubijeni snajperima što su pucali u svaki mogući dijelić grada sa obližnjih planinskih obronaka ili (kao u Pavinom slučaju) iz preostalih nebodera u samom gradu, prišla je da mi pomogne. Nisam znao da li je Pava vidjela opasnost.

"Žeteoče...", rekoh, pokazujući na čovjeka-duha koji je bio pored leša.

Nikada dosada, otkako sam dostigao ovo sablasno stanje, nijedan živi čovjek nije piljio u mene na takav način. I čak iako sam znao da je to zaista bio Žeteoc kojemu sam ja oduzeo pravo glasa, a ne čovjek uopšte, sve je bilo zastrašujuće. Čovjekovo lice je bilo osvijetljeno *strahom* i gnušanjem. Prvospomenuto je bio vjerovatno tračak psihe starog bića što je paničilo na sam dodir krvi. Na neki način smrtnik mora znati da ga je smrt dodirivala, iskorištavajući ga.

"Ova duša je spašena, Žeteoče." Uzeo sam ruku Djeteta i spremao se da odem, ali se iz grla čovjeka koji je bio u Žeteočevoj vlasti začuo šapat, šapat što proganja, i što je bio odgovor na moje riječi.

If the reaper could move the dying man to a position away from the devastation, perhaps behind or in the midst of the crowd where I or other Legionnaires would not see him, then he could steal away with an Enfant's soul as his prize. I could see no sign yet that this dead man might walk again after death, but I acted on the assumption that the reaper knew better.

The reaper started to move more quickly now. Vestigial *spasms* of life passed through the now dead man. I made certain that at least one of my comrades observed my pursuit before I attempted to negotiate a path on the reaper's heels. I avoided the crowd as best I could, but even so a few Sarajevans stumbled into me and caused some discomfort as I hurried to the corpse's side. But the reaper was also jarred by the crowd and he and his charge were knocked to the ground. Already, an Enfant was emerging from the corpse.

Because the reaper had possessed a living man and effectively became part of the realm of the living himself, he was beyond my reach. I could have attempted to cause harm to the mortal he possessed, but since I strove to protect the Sarajevans, I refused that option. Even so, it was a stalemate. I was beyond his reach as well. Fortunately, the Enfant was arriving on my side of the Shroud.

The reaper, I believe, was prepared to fight for his charge, but a fellow Legionnaire, Paša Sačić, an ethnic Croat among the first killed by the snipers who fired into every imaginable part of the city from the nearby mountainsides or (as in Paša's case) from the remaining high-rise buildings within the city itself, reached my side to back me up. I didn't know if Paša saw the danger.

"Reaper..." I said, indicating the ghostly man by the side of the corpse.

Never had a living man stared at me so since I achieved my ghostly state. And even though I knew it was really a reaper I'd disenfranchised and not just a man at all, it was horrifying. The man's face was lit with *fear* and disgust. The former was probably a glimmer of the psyche of the old who had panicked at the touch of blood. On some level the mortal must know that death was touching him, using him.

"This soul has been saved, reaper." I took the Enfant's hand and prepared to leave, but a haunting whisper rattled to my world from the throat of the reaper-possessed man.

I yearned to staunch the blood, to cut her open and compress the artery leaking her life away;
though in life I'd been a surgeon, I could do nothing. Now my work didn't begin until my patient was dead.

"Ovo je bio car Lazar, budalo!"

Naglo sam se okrenuo prema Žeteocu. Njegove oči su sijevale od ljutine.

Žeteoc je ponovo prozborio: "Poznajem te, Legionaru. Tvoja sudbina je sada Zaborav."

Ali nije se pomakao. Samo vreli, metalni, zakrvavljeni bljesak iz njegovih uskih očiju što me kupao u crvenom svjetlu. Okrenuo sam leđa Žeteocu i pažljivo odveo Dijete do Centuriona Gustičića koji se odmah pobrinuo za njega.

To je bio kraj našega spašavanja. Spašeno je više od desetak Djece. Nisam znao nizašta drugo nego za ovo visokoparno brojanje, ali Centurion mi je rekao da je prekomjerno visoki procenat umiranja na licu mjesta sada rezultirao postojanjem duhova u Sarajevu. Toliki životi su tragično završili. Ovi ljudi su imali i previše *strasti* za život što je ostala neizražena, da bi se preko toga tako jednostavno prešlo.

Preživio sam brodolom u ulici Vase Miskina i njegovo finale. Napokon su se Sarajlije mogli pobrinuti za ranjenike. Njihovi napori nisu bili osuđeni snjaperskom pucnjavom po onima koji su pokušavali spašavati ranjene ili pronaći mrtve.

Naše Rašćišćavanje je završeno, ali Sarajlije su tek sada počinjali da prebrojavaju svoje gubitke.

...

Bilo je kasno i patrola se razišla za to veče pa sam ja tumarao praznim ulicama Sarajeva. Centurion Gustičić nije odobravao da se mi sami šećemo, ali Lazareni su bili u mojim mislima i trebao sam da utvrdim da li bi me prijetnja tog gulikože trebala uzbuniti. Razmatrao sam to na način kako sam činio u životu: koračajući ulicama grada iako onda putevi nisu bili *zatrpani* djelićima stakla, komadima metala i grumenjem betona.

I mislio sam o Lazaru. Lazar!

"This one was Prince Lazar's, fool!"

I spun to face the reaper. His eyes were glowing a brilliant red.

The reaper whispered again, "I know you now, Legionnaire. Your destiny is now Oblivion."

But he made no move. Just the hot metal red from his narrow eyes that washed me with bloody light. I turned my back on the prone reaper and guided the Enfant carefully to Centurion Gustičić who immediately took charge of him.

It was the end of our rescue. More than a dozen Enfants saved. I knew nothing other than these kinds of inflated numbers, but the Centurion had told me an inordinately high percentage of mortal deaths resulted in ghosts in Sarajevo now. So many lives tragically cut short. These people had too many *passions* for life left unexpressed to simply pass on.

I surveyed the wreckage of Vaso Miskin Street a final time. At least the Sarajevans could tend their wounded. Their efforts were not thwarted by snipers firing at those who attempted rescues of the wounded or recovery of the dead. Such small respite is all that remains for them.

Our clean-up was done, but the Sarajevans were only beginning to count the losses.

...

It was late, and the patrol had disbanded for the evening, so I wandered the empty streets of Sarajevo. Centurion Gustičić didn't sanction wandering alone, but the Lazarians were on my mind and I needed to determine whether that skinrider's threat should alarm me. So I deliberated in the way I'd done during my life: by walking the streets of the city, though then the roads had not been *littered* with fragments of glass, scraps of metal, and chunks of concrete.

And I thought of Lazar. Lazar!

It was difficult though, because my new terrain mirrored Sarajevo, but it offered a skewed view.

Pretpostavljao sam da je "Lazarus" bilo porijeklo riječi takozvanih Lazarena, jedne od većih grupa duhova koji su odbili da se pripoje Hijerarhiji ali su ipak ostali da djeluju u Sarajevu. Združeno nazvane Odmetnucima, takve grupe su zapravo pravile više problema nego Žeteoci. Njihovo trajanje je, mislim, odredjivano njihovim medjusobnim sukobima a možda su te besmislene borbe uključivale i žive, takodje.

Ali oni su rekli "car" Lazar. Više smisla je bilo "Lazarus" - grupica odmetnika koja je osnovana na prepostavci iz priče kako je Isus povratio Lazara iz mrtvih. Bilo je prirodno, izgleda, za duhove da poštuju takvu priču.

Ali Lazar je bio neko potpuno drugi. Srpski *nacionalizam* u zadnjih nekoliko godina učinio je da se ne zaboravi taj ukleti, samoprozvani car i bitka na Kosovu, gdje je srpski plemić, car Lazar, poginuo u borbi prije nešto više od petsto godina.

Doista, to je bilo prije šesto godina i Lazar nije umro boreći se. Srpska poezija i legenda su prenapuhali bitku na Kosovu do epskog heroizma i duhovnog savršenstva što se sve završavalo time kako najbolje srpsko plemstvo umire braneći svoje balkanske zemlje od strahovitog napada zlikovačke otomanske vojske.

Znao sam sve ovo jako dobro jer je 28. juna 1989. godine bila šestogodišnjica bitke na Kosovu i proslavljena je sa mnogo gorljivosti i žara srpskih fanfara pored Prištine, na Kosovu, na bojištu Gazimestana, gdje se odvijao drevni okršaj. Ovo se desilo samo tri mjeseca nakon što je srpski parlament u martu 1989. donio rezoluciju kojom se ukidao nezavisni status Kosova stvarajući, zajedno sa drugom pokrajinom, Vojvodinom, prve nove komponente Velike Srbije. Prije nego što osobno kroči na ove svete zemlje, Slobodan Milošević, srpski vodja i istinski kreator bombardovanja Sarajeva, trebao je, očigledno, da posjeduje bojište gdje je njegov srpski car bio zarobljen i smaknut.

U mom duhovnom oku, iako se to činilo (a bukvalno i jeste bilo) udaljenim cio ljudski vijek, mogao sam vidjeti televizijsko izvještavanje o ovom dogadjaju. Ne ono kako su izvještavali službeni srpski mediji koji su portretisali dogadjaj kao Povratak Mesije na što je Milošević i ukazivao; nego bosansko izvještavanje što je pokazalo Miloševića koji je podbadao svjetinu svojom neozbiljnom *retorikom* a ostatku, Jugoslavije prijetio nasiljem. Ne sjećam se tačno svih riječi ali on je spominjao borbe koje Srbi vode i spomenuo je da te borbe nisu bile oružane, ali, ovoga dijela se mogu sjetiti zbog jeze koja mi je prošla kroz kičmu, "da se ni to ne može potpuno isključiti."

I'd assumed "Lazarus" was the root of the so-called Lazarians, one of the larger groups of ghosts that refused to affiliate with the Hierarchy but remained active in Sarajevo nonetheless. Collectively called Renegades, such groups were actually more trouble than the reapers. Their time, I thought, was dominated by their conflict with one another, but perhaps their ridiculous battles involved the living too.

But they said "Prince" Lazar. It made more sense as Lazarus — a band of Renegades established on some premise surrounding the return of Lazarus by the hand of Jesus. It seemed natural for ghosts to honor such a story.

But Lazar was someone else entirely. Serbian *nationalism* of a few years ago made it hard to forget that damnable self-proclaimed prince and the Battle of Kosovo where the Serbian noble, Prince Lazar, died fighting over five hundred years ago.

Actually, it was just over six hundred years ago, and Lazar didn't really die fighting. Serbian poetry and legend has exaggerated the Battle of Kosovo into an epic of heroism and spiritual accomplishment that concluded with the flowers of Serbian nobility dying while defending their Balkan lands against a juggernaut onslaught of the nefarious Ottoman army.

I knew this so well because June 28, 1989 was the six-hundredth anniversary of the Battle of Kosovo and it was celebrated with much fervor and Serbian fanfare near Priština, Kosovo, at the battlefield of Gazimestan, where the ancient conflict was waged. This, of course, was a mere three months after the Serbian Assembly in March 1989 passed a resolution that abolished the independent status of Kosovo and made it, along with another province, Vojvodina, the first new components of Greater Serbia. Before he would personally set foot upon those sacred lands, Slobodan Milošević, the Serb leader and the real architect of the bombardment of Sarajevo, apparently needed to possess the battlefield where his Serbian prince was captured and executed.

In my mind's eye, though it seemed (and was literally) a lifetime away, I could see the television coverage of the event. Not the official Serbian media, which cast the event as the Second Coming that Milošević suggested, but the Bosnian coverage that showed Milošević urging the crowd with puerile *rhetoric* and threatening the rest of Yugoslavia with violence. I don't remember all the exact words, but he mentioned the struggles facing Serbs and noted the battles were not armed, but that, and this part I recall because of the chill that ran down my spine, "this cannot be excluded yet."

Saint Vitus Dances Eternity

The implausibility, the seeming impossibility, of bombs dropping on children in the midst of their city is beyond their comprehension.

Milošević went on to forge the destiny of Yugoslavia. One that will likely claim hundreds of thousands of lives and also putrefy every moral and code of decency in order to wipe an entire race from the Balkans.

The disgusting display at Kosovo was all heralded by Prince Lazar. He was dead, yes (though what did that count for any longer in my reckoning!), but the *bones* of the Prince toured Serbia before the event, and images of Lazar were hoisted and sold in Gazimestan. Posters of Lazar sold beside those depicting Christ and, sickeningly, Milošević too.

I was shocked, and still am, that such an ancient event could be used to rouse such passionate hatred. Why is it that humankind's memory, usually so short and usually so ignorant of the past, could dredge up this event and clasp to it so? Why is everything most foul about the past imprinted indelibly in our collective memory? These mistakes occur again and again like a rolling wagon wheel — not only forever following itself but also forever mired in the same awful track.

Meanwhile, all that is good becomes a mere blip, a single spoke on that wheel that rises only to fall away again, forgotten.

If it's sins of the past he wishes to avenge, why doesn't Milošević wish to carve his Greater Serbia from Italy? As if that were truly his goal. After all, it was Diocletian who persecuted the Christians long before the Muslims, and it was during that emperor's ten-year massacre that the Serbs' beloved St. Vitus fell. June 28th is also the feast day of St. Vitus. Where is that in the rhetoric of Milošević?

Or is it there still? Is it just another anniversary of slaughtered Christians to be set at the feet of the people with the most convenient territory? Perhaps the spirit of that slaughtered Sicilian youth will never fade. And not just from Bosnia, but from the world over. Wherever there is a *lunatic* who will sagaciously tap-dance through history — here lingering on one event, there blithely skirting another — there will be people to dance with him.

Saint Vitus Dances Eternity

I surveyed the wreckage of Vaso Miskin Street a final time. At least the Sarajevans could tend their wounded.

Ali Lazar. Ubijen nakon svog poraza u rukama Otomanlija. Napregnuo sam se da se sjetim ko ga je pogubio. Nešto od pompezne mitologije ovog dogadjaja mi je pomoglo: bila je to armija Murata Prvoga. U bici na Kosovu, Murat Prvi je osvojio Srbiju u ime otomanskih Turaka, iako on sam nije bio prisutan da uživa u pobjedi. Srbin, koji se pretvarao da je dezerter, izvršio je na njega atentat prije završne bitke. Turčin je umro u svom šatoru, očekujući da od "dezertera" dobije obavještenja o srpskoj vojsci. Očigledno, ni nedostatak tih obavještenja niti gubitak sultana nisu načinili nikakav preokret.

I svaka osoba srpskoga porijekla zna, jer smo svi mi vjerovatno upoznati sa detaljima priče, da su Srbi zapravo izgubili zemaljsku bitku jer je pobožni Lazar previše volio svoj narod. Kaže se da se andjeo Ilija pojavio uoči završne bitke i ponudio Lazaru da izabere izmedju pobjede u ratu na zemlji i vječnosti u nebeskom kraljevstvu za sav njegov narod.

Pitam se je li Lazar *izmislio* ovu priču za one koji su bili pored njega u trenutku srpskoga poraza. Je li on napravio veliku taktičku grešku bojeći se da će ga njegovi ljudi ubiti prije nego što muslimanski osvajači dobiju priliku? Gubitak je mnogo lakše objasniti ukoliko je obojen obećanjima vječne pobjede.

Imao sam i drugu cinčnu pomisao na taj datum: 28. juni. To je bio dan 1914. godine kad je Gavrilo Princip izvršio atentat na nadvojvodu Franca Ferdinanda, nasljednika habsburškog prijestolja, u ulici Franca Jozefa u Sarajevu, čime su buknuli sukobi što će konačno progutati svijet kao Prvi svjetski rat.

Sve su ove misli uzburkavale moju uobrazilju. Moje *turobno* okruženje činilo je isto. Nisam mogao vjerovati u kakvu pustoš se Sarajevo pretvaralo. Samo nekoliko dana ranije hodao sam ovom istom ulicom u patroli, a sada se skoro sve izmijenilo. Bilo je više krša. Više zgrada je sravnjeno do zemlje. Više je rupa u visočijim, čvršćim zgradama, kao što je obližnja zgrada Oslobodjenja. I još nešto sam odmah shvatio: nema svjetla. Nije ponovo bilo struje. Za ljude iz Elektoprivrede, gradske elektro-službe, bila je to neprekidna borba posebne vrste. Oni su neprestano popravljali transformatorske stanice što su Srbi napadali, a kada je to napokon bilo popravljeno, oštećeni transformatorski toranj bi, negdje drugdje, oduzimao električnu rasvjetu drugom gradskom području, ako ne i cijelom gradu. Ili bi struja ponovo došla. Ponekad.

But Lazar. Killed after his defeat at the hands of the Ottomans. I strained my memory to recall his executioner. Some of the pompous mythology of the event helped. It was the army of Murat I. At the Battle of Kosovo, Murat I captured Serbia for the Ottomans, though he wasn't present to enjoy his victory. He was assassinated before the final clashes by a Serbian posing as a deserter. The Ottoman died in his own tent, where he expected to gain information about the Serbian army from the "deserter." The lack of information, and the loss of the sultan, apparently did nothing to turn the tide of the war.

But every person of Serb descent, for we are all probably familiar with these details of the story, knows that the Serbs actually lost the earthly battle because saintly Lazar loved his people so much. It's said that the angel Elijah appeared on the eve of the final battle and offered Lazar the choice between victory in the war on earth or else an eternity in the kingdom of heaven for all his people.

I wonder now if it was Lazar who *concocted* this story for those near him at the moment of the Serbian defeat. Did he make a great tactical blunder and fear his people would kill him before the conquering Muslims were given the opportunity? It's much easier to explain loss if it's colored by the promise of an eternal victory.

I had another wry thought about that date: June 28th. That was also the day in 1914 when Gavrilo Princip assassinated Archduke Franz Ferdinand, heir to the Hapsburg throne, on Franz Josef Street in Sarajevo to spark the conflicts that eventually engulfed the world as World War I.

All these thoughts stirred my imagination. My *dismal* surroundings did the same. I couldn't believe what a wasteland Sarajevo was becoming. I'd walked this street with the patrol no more than a few days ago, and already it was transformed. There was more debris. More buildings pounded flat. More holes in the taller, stronger buildings, like the nearby Oslobodjenje Building. And something else, I realized with a start: no lights. The electricity was out again. It was an ongoing battle of a different kind for the people of Elektroprivreda, the electrical utility company in the city. They were constantly repairing transformer stations the Serbs attacked, but once that was done a damaged transmission tower elsewhere would already have deprived another area of the city, if not the entire city, of electricity. The power would be back again. Sometime.

It was late, and the patrol had disbanded for the evening, so I wandered the empty streets of Sarajevo.

Planinski obronci koje su sada naseljavali Srbi postali su mnogo zlosutniji, takodje. Bez drveća i zgrada što su bile uništene granatiranjem, pa nisu zaklanjale vidik, njihova neublaživa militarna snaga je stajala otkrivena, mada su detalji bili prikriveni tamom.

Pitao sam se je li moj sin Kulin bio negdje u toj *tmini* čekajući da jurne na Srbe što su opkoljavali. Bio sam sa njim kad sam posljednji put hodao ovom ulicom u životu i , neizbježno, mislio sam uvijek na njega dok sam hodao istim uskim prolazom. Sada sam se pitao hoću li ga više ikada vidjeti na sarajevskim ulicama. Sumnjao sam. Sigurno da ga više nikada neću vidjeti živoga. Da je bio u Sarajevu, bio bi duh kao i ja. Ali sumnjao sam u to. Da je on poštojao u ovom zagrobnom životu, onda bi ga njegova sjećanja i žudnje zasigurno vezivali za bojišta Hercegovine ili za bilo koje drugo opustošeno mjesto gdje se zadnji put nalazio na položajima protiv Srba.

Naše postojanje je ovdje odista bilo u nekoj vrsti čistilišta. Ne znam da li možemo, našim akcijama na zemlji, promijeniti krajnju sudbinu ili izmijeniti neminovna odredišta, bilo da je to Raj ili Pakao, ali znam da mnogi to pokušavaju. Centurion Gustičić, zasigurno mora da vjeruje u ovo. Ima nešto u vezi njega, nešto što mogu otkriti samo podsvjesno i što me tjera da mislim da je ranije bio mnogo manje ljubazan nego što je sada. Mislim da on nastoji da izmijeni svoju sudbinu mijenjanjem svijeta u kojemu je prvobitno rodjen. Vjerovanje da možeš napraviti takve promjene na ovaj način ustrajava. Zbog toga sam mu zahvalan; inače bi ova planeta polako zarastala u istu tamu i isto zlo kao i svijet moga Sarajeva. To je bilo spiritualno bogatstvo koje obilježava pobjednika.

Misli su mi se vratile na mog jadnog Kulina. Fatima i ja smo mu dali ime sa takvim optimizmom. Željeli smo da njegovo vrijeme podsjeća, sa istom radošću, na doba kada je Bosna bila slobodna preko više od dvadeset godina, krajem dvanaestoga vijeka dok je bila pod vlašću Bana istog imena. To je bilo doba da se ponovo zaboravi *rasizam* ljudi kao što je moj otac, Srbin četnik, koji se borio pod vodjstvom generala Draže Mihajlovića, vodje "drugih" pobunjenih grupa tokom Drugog svjetskog rata. "Drugi" u odnosu na Titove komuniste koji su vladali Jugoslavijom u poslijeratnim godinama.

The mountainsides now populated by the Serbs were more ominous too. With intervening trees and buildings removed by the shelling, their implacable strength stood revealed, though the details were obscured by darkness.

I wondered if my son Kulin was poised somewhere out in that *darkness* to spring upon the encircling Serbs. It was with him that I last walked this street in life, and it was inevitably of him that I always thought when I walked its narrow way. Now I wondered if I would ever see him on the streets of Sarajevo. I doubted it. Certainly I would never again see him alive. If he was in Sarajevo, then it would be as a ghost like myself. But I doubted that too. If he existed in this afterlife, then his memories and passions would surely bind him to the battlefields of Herzegovina or whatever wasted place he made his last stand against the Serbians.

Here our existence was indeed a sort of purgatory. I don't know if we could change our eventual fate or alter our inevitable destination, be it Heaven or Hell, by our actions here, but I know that many try. Centurion Gustičić, for one, must believe this. Something about him, something I can only subliminally detect, makes me think he was once less kind than he is now. I think he seeks to change his fate by altering the world into which he was originally born. In this way the belief that you can make such changes persists. For that I am thankful; without it this land would slowly grow as dark and evil as the world of my Sarajevo. Here it is spiritual wealth that determines the victor.

My thought shifted back to my poor Kulin. Fatima and I named him with such optimism. We wanted his age to be one recalled centuries hence with the same joy as the time Bosnia was free for over twenty years at the close of the 12th Century under the Ban of the same name. It was time again to forget the *racism* of men like my father, the Četnik Serb who had fought under General Draža Mihailović, leader of the "other" rebel band during World War II. "Other" to Tito's Communists who came to dominate Yugoslavia's post-war years.

My thought shifted back to my poor Kulin. Fatima and I named him with such optimism.

Moj otac se razlikovao, ipak, na dosta načina, od generala kojemu se toliko divio. Najprije, on je bio zaveden tamo gdje general nije, srpskim nacionalističkim programima Vasića i Moljevića, koji, mislim, mora da su shvatili da je pometnja svjetskog rata bila najbolje doba da se otme zemlja za Srbe, bez obzira na milione Turaka, Hrvata i Jevreja koji su takodje živjeli ovdje. Ne bi bilo ništa gore ni da je *solona* Milošević bio mi otac. Proveo sam dio moje odmetničke mladosti zaveden komunizmom samo zbog toga jer je moj otac prezirao Tita. Onda sam otkrio da je Tito bio i sam masovni ubojica, iako mu je, čudnovato, svijet, još prije njegove smrti 1980. godine, dozvolio da postane domaćinom Zimskih olimpijskih igara u 1984. Ali odista, to ne iznenadjuje jer isti svijet dozvoljava ono što se sada dešava u Sarajevu.

A što se tiče Fatime, ona je željela da izbriše sjećanje na vlastitog oca. Možda što nisam bio izložen njegovom licemjerju iz dana u dan, pa ne mogu koriti Ahmeda Popovca kao što mogu svoga oca. Moj otac je bio budala uskih pogleda koji je odbijao da nešto razmotri sa strane da bi mu to postalo jasnije. Ahmed je bio samo slabić. Savjesno je prihvatio Titove stroge zakone protiv Muslimana, kao što je nasilno skidanje vela muslimanskim ženama 1950. godine, iste godine kada je bila rodjena moja supruga. Samo osam godina kasnije Ahmed Popovac je odustao od svoje religije da bi se uklopio sa (ili kako bi Fatima rekla "dodvorio") komunističkim vodjama u Jugoslaviji. Dvije godine nakon toga, 1960. godine, skoro jedanaest godina nakon što su mnogi od njegovih saradnika i prijatelja u "Mladim Muslimanima" bili zatvoreni zbog otpora komunističkom zatiranju islamske vjeroispovijesti, Ahmed Popovac je postao dio jugoslovenskog diplomatskog tijela na Bliskom Istoku.

Ahmed je uzrujavao Fatimu stepenom njegovog zadovoljstva našim brakom 1969. godine. Ona je bila svjesna da je njegovo trenutačno odobrenje bilo zato jer ja nisam bio Musliman i veza sa mnom, Srbinom, donosila bi, po Ahmedovom mišljenju, dosta opravdanja u modernoj Jugoslaviji. A Fatima nije nikada oprostila ocu grdnju kad ga je obavijestila da je ona insistirala da bude upisana drugačije nego ja u popisu iz 1971. godine izjašnjavajući se kao "Musliman, u smislu nacije." Predložio sam da i ja budem isto tako upisan, kao znak solidarnosti, ali je ona s pravom insistirala da je snaga Bosne u njenoj *raznolikosti* i mnoštvu nacionalnih identiteta, pa sam se ja ubilježio kao Srbin.

Kulin je bio rodjen te iste godine. Upisali smo ga kao Srbina jer nije bilo opcije "Bosanac," a to je bio izbor koji bi prouzrokovao najmanje rasprava sa našim očevima. Obadvojica su, naravno, bili zadovoljni.

My father, though, was in many ways unlike the general he so admired. Foremost, he was tempted where the general was not by the Serbian nationalist agenda of Vasić and Moljević, whom I think must have felt that the confusion of the World War was the best time to seize lands for the Serbs, no matter the millions of Turks and Croats and Jews who lived here too. It could have been no worse had the *devil* Milošević been my father. I spent part of my rebellious youth seduced by Communism simply because my father despised Tito. Then I discovered that Tito was a mass murderer himself, though strangely the world still granted him the 1984 Winter Olympics before his death in 1980. But not so surprisingly really, as this is the same world that allows Sarajevo now.

And for her part, Fatima wished to erase memories of her own father. Perhaps it's because I was not exposed to his hypocrisy day after day, but I cannot fault Ahmed Popovac as I can my father. My father was a close-minded fool who refused even to use hindsight to make his vision clearer. Ahmed was just a weak man. He accepted Tito's harsh laws against the Muslim faithful, like the forcible unveiling of Muslim women in 1950, the very year that my wife was born. It was only eight years later that Ahmed Popovac gave up his religious faith to integrate (or as Fatima would say, "ingratiate") himself with the Communist rulers of Yugoslavia. Two years after that, in 1960, a mere eleven years after many of his associates and friends in the "Young Muslims" were imprisoned for resisting the Communist annihilation of the Islamic faith, Ahmed Popovac was part of the Yugoslavian diplomatic corps in the Middle East.

Ahmed upset Fatima with the degree of his delight in our marriage in 1969. She felt his instant approval of the arrangement was because I was not Muslim, and association with me, a Serb, would win her even more accord in modern Yugoslavia. And Fatima never forgave her father's scolding when she informed them that she had insisted on being listed differently than me in the 1971 census. She classified herself as "Muslim, in the sense of a nation." I suggested that I be listed the same as a show of solidarity, but she rightly insisted that the strength of Bosnia was in its *diversity* and variety of ethnic personalities, so I noted myself as Serbian.

Kulin was born in that same year. We listed him as Serbian, because there was no option for "Bosnian," and because that was the choice that would cause the least dispute with our fathers. Both, of course, were delighted.

Saint Vitus Dances Eternity

Was this harrowing landscape the result of a promised land not to Lazar's liking? Was he here leading the Lazarians and trying to reclaim the physical landscape he'd ignorantly forsaken in exchange for this purgatory of grey?

But Kulin's life would not go as pleasantly as either of us hoped, or, I'm certain, we so fervently believed it would. He grew up the product of a multi-ethnic society. It was one, of course, that didn't encourage diversity, but options were still there. Something in him, though, sensed the injustice done to Alija Izetbegović, a former "Young Muslim" and future President of Bosnia, when in 1983 Izetbegović was prosecuted for pro-Muslim activity.

After that, Kulin was wary for signs of political *turmoil*. He didn't begin to associate with the Muslims even now so much as he disassociated with the Serbs. And this was especially true with the rise of Slobodan Milošević and his speech in 1989. Not long after that, Kulin flew the nest. Fatima's death by cancer later in 1989 — thank God she missed this hell! — certainly precipitated his departure, but his own motives and passions were fully formed as a young man of nineteen, and he joined the Party for Democratic Action, Izetbegović's SDA, in 1990.

I celebrated beside him on the streets of Sarajevo just a few months ago in March. We walked this route the next day. We stopped here, I realized as I stopped my walk again, at this now burnt out hull of a café for *ćevapi*, Turkish coffee served in beautiful *fildjans*, and just a sip of that wonderful brandy, *lozovača*. I was hopeful, but he was fearful, and eventually his worries broke me down too. I spoke with Kulin as parents should speak with their children sometimes. We spoke of many things, and I hold those moments in my heart as my last words with my son. I do not have regrets that anything in my life with him, my life for him, was left unexpressed.

Before the end of the month he was gone to defend any number of villages against the assault of Milošević and Karadžić's Serbs. I only knew he was gone by a brief message on my phone machine. It was all he needed to say.

I wonder if he knew I was dead. That I was killed less than a month later? Or that one week earlier I had *buried* my father? I'd smiled ironically on Kulin's behalf when his grandfather was killed by a Serbian shell. More Serbs die every day at the hands of those who claim to wish to liberate them. I wonder if they cared that they had put down a WWII Četnik.

Saint Vitus Dances Eternity

The shelling of my once beautiful city was unending.
Not a single day passed without more shelling, which made it over two months of constant terror and death for the residents of the Sarajevo.

I tako sam lutao umirućim ulicama grada do zore. Život ne zablista pred čovjekom tek u smrti, nego i bezbroj puta poslije smrti, takodje. Ali sa izlazećim sunčevim zracima sinulo mi je u glavi, pošto tiho razmišljanje noći donosi svoj rezultat. Možda je to bila samo moja mašta ali vodja druge glavne frakcije Otpadnika bio je Turčin, možda Otomanlija. Je su li mrtvi nosili takvu mržnju, takvo životinjsko neprijateljstvo, kao i živi? Da li se kobni točak istorije okreće u beskraj čak i medju mrtvima?

Je li ovaj pejsaž što para srce ishod obećane zemlje, ali ne po Lazarevom ukusu? Je li on bio ovdje predvodeći Lazarene i pokušavajući da povrati materijalni pejsaž kojega se neupućeno *odrekao* u zamjeni za ovo čistilište tame?

...

Mjesec je prošao dok sam saznao nešto više. Granatiranje mog nekada prelijepoga grada nije prestajalo. Nije bilo ni jednog jedinoga dana da prodje bez granatiranja, što je već preko dva mjeseca donosilo neprestani teror i smrt za stanovnike Sarajeva.

Nevjerovatno, Hijerarhija je bila još jedina snaga što je izgledalo da se o bilo čemu brine. Naše kopije u živom kraljevstvu bili su Plavi šljemovi UNPROFOR-a, koji su nekada radosno pozdravljani i kojima su *stanovnici* Sarajeva nekada klicali. Sada su bili samo predmet prezira. Upravo sam posmatrao mladoga čovjeka kako - uprkos neprestanoj paljbi srpskih ubojica - žuri prema drugom čovjeku koji je bio pogodjen snajperskim hicem sa zadnjega sprata neke napuštene zgrade. Mladi čovjek, civil, možda pekar ili čistač dimnjaka, riskirao je svoj život; Plavi šljem je stajao i posmatrao dvadesetak koraka dalje. Kada je pucnjava postala žešća, mladi heroj je bio prinudjen da se povuče.

Poslije mnogo dodvoravanja i mnogo vremena, mladi čovjek je ubijedio Plavca da dokotrlja njihova blindirana kola desetak koraka unazad kako bi mu osigurao zaklon pri pokušaju spašavanja. Tridesetak minuta kasnije, ranjeni čovjek je bio mrtav, a ja, ostavši tu po naredjenju Centuriona Gustičića, čekao sam da vidim sudbinu čovjekove Duše. On je transcendirao, prešao je u drugi svijet.

Možda je mogao stići do bolnice i preživjeti, da je Plavi šljem imao samo tračak humanosti - toliko da malo brže predje preko pravila neintervenisanja koje svi krše.

And so it was that I wandered the dying streets of the city until dawn. A life does not flash before one only at death, but countless times after death as well. Yet with the rising sunlight there was also a flash in my mind as the silent ruminations of the night bore fruit. Perhaps it was just my imagination, but the leader of the other major faction of Renegades was a Turk, maybe an Ottoman. Did the dead bear such hatred, such animal animosity, as the living? Did the ominous wheel of history endlessly roll even among the dead?

Was this harrowing landscape the result of a promised land not to Lazar's liking? Was he here leading the Lazarians and trying to reclaim the physical landscape he'd ignorantly *forsaken* in exchange for this purgatory of grey?

...

A month passed before I learned more. The shelling of my once beautiful city was unending. Not a single day passed without more shelling, which made it over two months of constant terror and death for the residents of the Sarajevo.

Unbelievably, the Hierarchy was still the only force that seemed to give a damn. Our counterparts in the living realm, the Blue Helmets of UNPROFOR, once cheered and cherished by the *inmates* of Sarajevo, were now the object of contempt. Just now I've watched a young man — despite the continuing fire of the Serb assassin — hurry to the side of another man sniped from the top floors of an abandoned apartment building. The young man, a civilian, perhaps a baker or chimney sweep, risked his life, while twenty paces away a Blue Helmet stood and watched. When the shooting became heavier the young hero was forced to retreat.

Only after much cajoling and much time did the young man convince the Blue Helmet to roll his armored car ten paces backward to provide cover for his rescue efforts. Thirty minutes later the wounded man was dead, and I, left behind at Centurion Gustičić's order, waited to see the fate of the man's soul. He transcended.

He might have made it to a hospital and survived if the Blue Helmet had possessed just a sliver of humanity — just enough to a bit more quickly bend the non-intervention rules they all break.

Saint Vitus Dances Eternity

Bilo je to prvi put da sam mogao zastati dovoljno dugo da budem svjedokom transcendencije. Drugi, kojima sam pripomagao, i ranije su transcendirali ali uvijek dok sam ja bio u patroli. U takvim prilikama nije bilo dovoljno vremena da se uživa u ovom čudesnom dogadjaju. Bio sam suviše zaposlen jureći u narednu zgradu koju je gutala vatra ili jureći prema sljedećem odrpanom lešu.

Ali sada sam posmatrao. Izgledalo je da čovjek ne tone u sebe, kao što neki čine prije putovanja preko granice izmedju života i ove ravni duhova. Umjesto toga, činilo se da se ovaj čovjek uvećava. Bilo je to metafizičko poredjenje kao kada slijepa osoba progleda po prvi put - prvi iznenadni šok kada se misli da je sve to previše i da bi bilo bolje ponovo biti slijep. Ali tada je dolazila radost, kao neopterećeno spajanje sa nadahnutom ljubavi, kad je on bio sposoban da prepozna vidokrug djelovanja ali nije bio posve sposoban da odgonetne ovu *beskonačnost*. Onda, polagano, dolazila je velika zapanjenost kad se shvati kako da se izrazi ovaj geštalt kosmosa. Ili možda satisfakcija da se to više i ne treba da zna.

Mogao sam vidjeti jedino samog čovjeka, naravno, a ne sve ono s čime se on susretao ili što je razmišljao. Dok sam ga posmatrao, on je zadrhtao, iznenadno se okrenuvši, na što sam se ja protresao od jeze. Sunčeva svjetlost se prelamala u kružnim šarama i progutala ga je.

Nastavio sam dalje, zavideći čovjeku na osjećaju sveprisutnosti kojega je on, izgleda, zadobio. Nisam imao još mnogo slobodnog vremena. Trebao sam da se sretnem sa patrolom u takozvanoj Aleji snajpera, što je ranije bila ulica Vojvode Putnika, glavni bulevar u Sarajevu koji se pružao kroz cijeli grad. Tu su srpski snajperisti imali relativno čist pregled na Sarajlije po ulicama. Ovdje ljudi nisu bili uhvaćeni uništavanjem granatama iz minobacača što nisu imale nikakvu posebnu metu, nego su bili direktno na nišanu. Nikako nisam mogao shvatiti kako *čudovište* može namjerno pucati na civile, muškarce i žene i, da, na djecu takodje, i pri tome se zvati ratnikom ili vojnikom.

Hijerarhija je neprestano patrolirala na ovom području jer su mrtvi bili neizbježni. Oblast je bila puna duhova bez uma, što su posjećivali mjesto njihove smrti.

Požurio sam dolje sjevernom stranom rijeke Miljacke. Nije prošlo dugo kad sam vidio zgradu Oslobodjenja u plamenu. Kučkini sinovi su je se konačno domogli. Plamenovi su se snažno razgorijevali u svakom od dva identična desetokatna zdanja, ali znamenitost koja je po završetku radova smatrana najmodernijom zgradom u Sarajevu, izgledala je da će ipak preživjeti pa makar samo kao skelet od betona i čelika.

It was the first time I was able to pause long enough to actually witness transcendence. Others I administered had transcended before, but always when I was on patrol. In such instances there was not enough time to appreciate this miraculous event. I was too busy racing into the next fire-gutted building or to the side of the next tattered corpse.

But now I watched. The man seemed not to sink into himself as one does before the journey across the barrier between life and this ghostly plane. Instead, he appeared to expand. It was the metaphysical parallel to a blind person seeing for the first time — that first instant of shock when he thought it was too much and that it would be better to be blind again. But then came a bliss, like the unburdening union of inspirational love, when he was able to ken the scope of everything, but was not nearly capable of deciphering this *infinity*. Then, slowly, came the heady amazement of realizing how to express the universe's gestalt. Or perhaps a satisfaction at no longer needing to know.

I could only observe the man himself, of course, not whatever he was encountering or contemplating. As I watched, he shuddered through a sudden twisting that sent shivers of vertigo through me. The sunlight refracted in circuitous patterns and swallowed him.

I moved on, envious of the omnipresence the man seemed to gain. I didn't have that much time to spare. I was to meet the patrol along so-called Sniper Alley, formerly Vojvode Putnika, which was the main cross-town boulevard in Sarajevo. It was here that the Serb snipers had a relatively clear view of Sarajevans on the streets. It was here that people were specifically targeted, instead of caught in the random destruction of a mortar shell. How a *monster* could purposely shoot civilian men and women and, yes, children too, and call himself a warrior, or even a soldier, was beyond my understanding.

The Hierarchy made constant patrols of the area because deaths were inevitable. The area was also thick with mindless ghosts haunting the site of their deaths.

I hurried down the northern bank of the Miljacka River. It was not long before I saw that the Oslobodjenje Building was in flames. The bastards had finally gotten it. The flames were burning hard in each of the twin ten-story towers, but the landmark that was hailed upon its completion as the most modern building in Sarajevo looked like it would yet survive — if only as a skeleton of steel and concrete.

Sveti Vito Pleše za Vječnost

Pitao sam se da li je Kemal Kurspahić bio unutra. Nadao sam se da su glavni urednik i ekipa koja se odazvala njegovom pozivu da nastave sa radom, bili neozlijedjeni. Novine "Oslobodjenje," kako je i zgrada dobila ime, po originalnom nazivu novina iz 1943. godine kada su Titovi partizani štampali novine na pokretnim presama, su se još uvijek štampale svaki dan, a 10,000 dostupnih kopija je odmah rasprodavano.

Glas novina nije samo da pozove na oružje nego i protiv *zločina*, što je bio stav koji je prevladavao u vrijeme moje smrti. Naravno, to je bilo prije nešto više od mjesec dana. Već predugo da sebi ponovo predočim porodjajne bolove onoga što naštoji da živi. Da jednostavno preživi! Sada sam jedino morao da postojim. Puno lakše! Manje pitanja da se odgovori, bar zasada.

Pokušao sam da se skoncentrišem na neposredno okruženje ali zgrada u plamenu je zaokupila moju pažnju. Onda sam čuo snajperske hice što su prštali iz gornjih dijelova zgrade - sa spratova koji su bili u plamenu, mislim. Vjerovatno da bi se obeshrabrili spasioci ili napori vatrogasaca. Patrola je već bila u zgradi, sigurno! Znao sam da će Hijerarhija reagovati. To me je umirilo i ponovo sam počeo nadgledati ulicu.

Prošao sam pored nekoliko kola koja su bila napuštena na ulicama. Haube automobila su bile otvorene. Pala mi je na pamet stara navika da se ovo pripiše huliganima, prije nego što sam shvatio da se pljačka samo nekoliko odredjenih predmeta, a posebno baterije iz kola. Nestanci struje su bili tako uobičajeni i dugotrajni pa su ljudi tragali za bilo kakvim sredstvima da opskrbe energijom rasvjetu i ostala pomagala.

Na drugoj strani ulice zamijetio sam nešto čudnovato: prodavnica metalne robe koja je još otvorena. Kakva vrsta mušterija, pitao sam se, bi mogla biti u potrazi za materijalima da nanovo izgrade njihove opustošene domove. Krov same prodavnice je bio napuknut, metar duboka pukotina. Ali kada sam prolazio vidio sam da je unutra zaista bilo mušterija. Ljudi koji su očajnički nastojali da održe osjećaj normalnosti.

Dok sam prilazio na otprilike pola kilometra od UNPROFOR-ovog sjedišta, iza kojega je bila još uvijek plamteća zgrada Oslobodjenja, bio sam svjedokom veoma obeshrabrujuće nagodbe. Bila je to crna berza u djelovanju. Dva čovjeka su stajala ispred mene u aleji što je bila uvučena podalje od ceste. Jedan je bio nonšalantan i izgledalo je kao da je zaboravio na ratno okruženje, dok se drugi žacao pri svakome odjeku topovske paljbe u daljini i skoro se bacio na zemlju kad je čuo kako granata *eksplodira* u blizini. Prvi, izgleda, nije bio uznemiren, nimalo zbunjen.

I wondered if Kemal Kurspahić was inside. I hoped the editor-in-chief and the crew that responded to his call to continue the paper were unharmed. The newspaper "Liberation", for which the building was named because of the paper's origins in 1943 when Tito's militiamen printed it from mobile presses, was still printed every day, and the 10,000 available copies always sold out instantly.

The voice of the paper is one not purely of alarm, but of *outrage*, which I think was the predominant emotion at least at the time of my death. Of course, that was more than a month ago. Almost too long for me to still imagine the travails of trying to live. To simply survive! Now I only had to exist. So much easier! So far fewer questions to answer.

I tried to concentrate on my immediate surroundings, but the burning building dominated my attention. Then I heard sniper fire rattling into the upper reaches of the building — at the floors in flame, I thought. Probably to discourage rescue or firefighting efforts. Surely a patrol was already in the building! I knew the Hierarchy would respond. That calmed me, and I watched the street again.

I passed a number of cars abandoned in the streets. The hoods were mostly propped open. The old reaction of attributing this to vandals jumped to mind before I realized that only a few items were being stripped, and one in particular: the car batteries. The power outages were frequent and often long, so people were searching for any means of powering their lights, stoves, and other appliances.

On the other side of the street I soon noted an oddity: a hardware store still open. What manner of customers, I wondered, would possibly be in search of material to rebuild their devastated homes? The roof of the store itself was torn by a meter-long gash. But as I passed I saw that there were indeed customers within. People desperately trying to maintain a sense of normality.

As I came within about a quarter-mile of the UNPROFOR headquarters, just a scoot beyond which was the still burning Oslobodjenje Building, I witnessed a very discouraging transaction. It was the black market in operation. Two men stood ahead of me in an alley recessed from the street. One was nonchalant and seemed oblivious to the war-torn surroundings, while the other flinched with every rattle of gunfire in the distance and almost threw himself to the ground when he heard a shell *detonate* in the distance. The first didn't seem perturbed at all.

Taj čovjek je očigledno kontrolisao situaciju i uživao je u tome. Njegova čekinjasta brada, razuzdana tetovaža a posebno sijevajuće i zlobne male oči obilježile su ga u mojoj glavi kao hulju. Tip mladog čovjeka koji je prije rata živio na rubu društva. Tip koji samo čeka na *lakiranje* civilizacije kojoj su trebale hiljade godina da se izgradi i da bi opet bila ogoljena tako da je svako mogao postojati u takvom kraljevstvu - u svijetu gdje je on mogao biti gospodar.

Nervozni, stariji čovjek je nabavljao cigarete od "trgovca" iako je bilo jasno da u tome nije uživao. Izgledao je kao tip pažljivog, intelektualnog čovjeka koji je nekada imao poziciju u društvu, zadobivenu vremenom i naporom. Sada je njegova pozicija bila preokrenuta. Zamislio sam ovo dvoje kao bivšeg studenta i profesora. Nekadašnji profesor koji je obarao na ispitima buntovnog mladića, a sada je od njega zavisio da dobije brzi udisaj nikotina.

Imao sam ironičnu predstavu o ovim ljudima kao o dva lica Radovana Karadžića, političkog vodje nacionalistički orijentisanih bosanskih Srba. Došao je u Sarajevo kao sirovi dječak sa planine i tražio je sve šanse za promociju u društvo kojem nije pripadao. Da bi ušao u to društvo postao je profesor - jedva da vjerujem svojim sjećanjima da je on bio stalni profesor psihijatrije na sarajevskom univerzitetu ili klubski ljekar fudbalskog tima Sarajevo. Ali onda je on povratio svoje staro lice. Lice čovjeka koji je želio da bude kralj čak iako je to značilo uništavanje civilizacije da bi se to dogodilo.

Pokušao sam da zamislim da je on bio pronicljiv čovjek koji je upotrebljavao psihijatrijske trikove da preobrati mišljenje i vjerovanja ljudi koji su ga pratili. Ali to je bilo uzalud. Jedini trikovi, za koje je bio sposoban, bili su oni najobičniji, kao na primjer njegova tvrdnja da je bio zatvaran kao politički zatvorenik, dok je presuda zapravo bila u vezi skandala oko kredita za kuću.

Bilo je tu nešto više oko ove razmjene na ulici što me je prenerazilo: cijena. Mogao sam jasno vidjeti kako se izmjenjuju novčanice dok sam se približavao ovoj dvojici. Profesor je platio više od hiljadu dinara za kutiju cigareta! To je u potpunosti iznosilo jednu desetinu prosječne penzije od 10,000 dinara na mjesec!

Zatresao sam glavom u *očajanju*. Možda bi cijena bila manja da je čovjek bio sposoban da plati u dolarima. Inflacija kod nas nije nikada bila posve pod kontrolom, ali ovo je bilo apsurdno. Svaki dinar što je crnoberzijanac prihvatao, vjerovatno je gubio vrijednost istog momenta.

The patient man was clearly in control and enjoying it. His stubble of a beard, wild tattoos, and especially his gleaming and malicious little eyes marked him in my mind as a likely miscreant. The kind of young man who lived on the fringes of society before the war. The kind just waiting for the *veneer* of civilization that's taken thousands of years to build up to be stripped away so everyone could exist in his realm — a world in which he could be the master.

The nervous, older man was purchasing cigarettes from the "merchant," though he was clearly not enjoying it. He looked the sort of intent, intellectual man who had once occupied a position in society won with time and effort. Now his position was reversed. I imagined the two as former student and professor. Where once the professor flunked the unruly youth, now he was dependent on him for a quick stroke of nicotine.

I had an ironic vision of these men as the two faces of Radovan Karadžić, the political leader of the Bosnian Serb nationalists. He came to Sarajevo from the mountains as a young boy, rough and looking for chances of promotion into a society to which he did not belong. To enter it he became a professor — I could hardly believe my memories of him as a tenured professor of Psychiatry at the University of Sarajevo or as the team doctor for the Sarajevo Football Club. But then he put the old face back on. That of a man driven to be a king, even if it meant that civilization had to be torn down to make it so.

I tried to imagine he was a smart man who used devious psychiatric tricks to twist the thoughts and beliefs of the men who followed him. But it was in vain. The only tricks I could imagine him capable of were the most ordinary ones, like his claim that he was once imprisoned as a political prisoner when his sentence was truly for a scandal involving home loans.

But there was more about this exchange on the streets that staggered me: the price. I could clearly see the bills being exchanged as I drew nearer the two. The professor paid more than a thousand dinars for a pack of cigarettes! That was fully one-tenth of the average pension of 10,000 dinars a month!

I shook my head in *dismay*. Perhaps the price would have been less had the man been able to pay in dollars. Our inflation had never really been under control, but this was ridiculous. Each dinar the black marketeer accepted probably lost value every moment.

Sveti Vito Pleše za Vječnost

Mogao sam se sjetiti vremena, samo nekoliko godina ranije, kada su se za isti dinarski iznos mogle kupiti cigarete u vrijednost od preko pedest američkih dolara. No pretpostavljam, ovo je bila ekonomija ratnog doba. Čovjek nije izgledao kao neko ko ima porodicu, pa u najmanju ruku, ta desetina od njegove moguće mjesečne zarade nije neizbježno bila potrošena na sledovanje ili kruh. Ipak, to me je posve dojmilo kao potpun apsurd.

Nastavio sam svojim putem, praveći široki zavoj oko prevrnutih i izgranatiranih uličnih kola.

Konačno, prošao sam pored zgrade Oslobodjenja. Nisam našao nikakav znak hijerahijske patrole ali sam znao da neka od njih mora da je unutra. Ostao sam svjestan da je zgrada gorjela iza mene čak i kada sam izašao iz njene sjenke.

Poslije kratkog vremena, prešao sam Miljacku i ušao sam na glavnu raskrsnicu duž Aleje snajpera. Svuda okolo vidio sam ljude kako su se *šćućurili* uza zidove. Uglavnom su se bili stisnuli uz zidove zgrada na južnoj strani ulice jer je najviše teške artiljerije bilo u brdima južno od grada, pa je ovo bio način da se ljudi bar malo više zaštite. Naravno, sigurnost je nalagala da ostanu u svojim kućama ali gladna djeca i saznanje da su njihovi domovi potencijalne mete za nasumično srpsko nasilje, prinudjavali su ih na ulice. I oni su trebali da prelaze ove raskrsnice.

Poslovni čovjek koji je ščepao aktovku i brzo trčao preko ulice.

Mladić na nekoj nepoznatoj misiji vratio se da zauzme start za trčanje i jurnuo je u dijagonali preko raskrsnice. Bila je to veća razdaljina ali je spasen prelaska dva raskršća.

Žena pored mene je nosila dvije vekne hljeba i izrekla je kratku i gotovo nečujnu molitvu prije nego što je energičnog pretrčala preko.

Na južnoj strani ulice, mladi čovjek u farmericama i majici je mijenjao položaj nogu na odredjeni način, za dobru sreću, prije no što je jurnuo na ulicu. Sve više i više sam vidio kako ljudi zavise na *praznovjerju* i nadi da ih brane od bezumnosti.

Posmatrati ove ljude bilo je kao da gledam neki rani crno-bijeli film. Kretali su se užurbano kao Čarli Čaplin ili Baster Kiton kada ih slijedi smotani policajac. Sarajevski ambijent je bio nešto drugačiji, ipak. To je bila kombinacija Čarli Čaplina i ratnih filmskih žurnala iz četrdesetih. Kiton koji je luckasto poigravao oko ruševina zgrada što su poharane vatrom ili srušene. Grotesno lijepo.

I could recall a time just a few years ago when that same amount of dinars would have bought well over fifty U.S. dollars of cigarettes. That, I suppose, was a war-time economy. The man didn't look the sort to have a family, so at least that tenth of his possible monthly earnings wasn't necessarily better spent on rations or bread. Still, it struck me as ridiculous.

I resumed my walk, making a large loop around a capsized and shell-shocked streetcar.

Finally, I passed by the Oslobodjenje Building. I saw no evidence of a Hierarchy patrol, but I knew one must be inside. I remained very aware of it burning behind me even as I passed out of its shadow.

Just a short time later I crossed the Miljacka and entered a major intersection along Snipers' Alley. Everywhere around me I saw people *huddled* against walls. Mostly they were pressed against the buildings on the south side of the street, for most of the heavy guns were in the hills south of the city, so this was one means people had of seeking a little extra protection. Of course, safety bade them to remain in their homes, but hungry children and a knowledge that their homes were also potential targets of random Serb violence compelled them to the streets. And they needed to cross these intersections.

A business man clutched his briefcase to his back and sprinted across the street.

An adolescent boy on some unknown mission backed up to get a running start and darted diagonally across the intersection. It was a greater distance, but it saved two crossings.

From near me a woman toting two loaves of bread said a short and almost silent prayer before hustling across.

And on the south side, a young man in jeans and T-shirt shuffled his feet in a repeating pattern for good luck before dashing into the street. More and more I observed a dependence on such *superstitions* and hopes as a defense against insanity.

Watching these people was like viewing an early black and white movie. They moved in hurried blurs like Charlie Chaplin or Buster Keaton when pursued by incompetent policemen. The setting in Sarajevo was a little bit different, though. It was Chaplin mixed with a 1940s war newsreel. Keaton prancing madly about the ruins of gutted and torn buildings. Grotesquely beautiful.

It was not long before I saw that the Oslobodjenje Building was in flames.

Usred sve ove jurnjave nisam odmah otkrio zakukuljenog duha što je polako hodao prema sredini raskršća. Ovaj novi žitelj zemlje mrtvih se ponašao sa rijetkom posvećenošću zadatku, za nekoga ko je još uvijek bio u košuljici. Ovaj duh je bila žena i sudeći po smrtnim obilježjima koja su još uvijek bila na njoj, i njenim ustima što su bilo široko otvorena i borila se za dah u ovom bezzračnom prostoru, pretpostavljao sam da je umrla *gušenjem*. Možda je bila uhvaćena ispod hrpe ruševina kakve nastaju kada granata eksplodira u blizini.

Gledao sam je zbunjeno. Šta je to ona radila?

Ženine oči su bile široko otvorene i napete i jedva vidljive kroz izmaglicu njene košuljice. Izgledalo je da je ona nešto odlučila i kada se zaustavila u sredini raskršća i podigla njene ruke visoko iznad glave, iznenada sam shvatio da je znala gdje se nalazi. Fizički, svakako, ako ne u metafizičkom smislu. Psihotične i višebojne slike koje su je sigurno proganjale nakon što je uskrsnula poslije smrti, nadvladjivale su njenu pomućenu snagu.

Ukoliko smrt nije bila dovoljna, onda će vas zagrobni život dovesti do ludila. Kao što je skoro bio slučaj sa mnom, sve dok me nije pronašao Centurion Gustičić.

A ova žena, misleći da je još uvijek živa i hodajući Snajperskom alejom u Sarajevu, počinjavala je samoubistvo - samoubistvo u sarajevskom stilu. Nudila se snajperistima u planinama iznad grada. Niko nije pucao, naravno, jer ljudi koje je ona mogla vidjeti, nisu nju mogli vidjeti, a kamoli je zamisliti. Bila je preplavljena slikama iz prošlosti, sadašnjosti i budućnosti koje su je proganjale i to joj je *pomutilo* um jer ih je prihvatala kao stvarnost. Sve zbog toga što je patrola nije pronašla. Sve dosada.

Nisam znao gdje je moja patrola. Možda su skrenuli prema zgradi Oslobodjenja. Ako je tako, drago mi je što im se nisam pridružio, jer ne bih nikada spasio ovu ženu.

Posmatrajući, doduše, izmicala je šansa da je spasim. Dok sam ja stajao iznenadjen, gledajući je kako se uzaludno žrtvuje naoružanim strijelcima koji je nisu mogli ubiti, Žeteoc se ustremio prema ženi. Prije nego što sam ga mogao opomenuti ili upozoriti ženu, ona je već bila sputana i uhvaćena u okove.

Zurio sam, omamljen, a onda sam konačno izazvao mog protivnika. "Žeteoče! Pusti je! Ona je pod zaštitom Hijerarhije."

Amid all of this scurrying I was slow to detect the cauled ghost that walked slowly to the center of the intersection. For one still cauled, this new denizen of the land of the dead was acting with rare dedication to her task. The ghost was indeed a woman, and from the deathmarks still plain upon her, and a mouth that was yet wide open and gasping for breath in this airless land, I guessed she'd died by *asphyxiation*. Perhaps she'd been trapped under a pile of rubble of the kind that results when a shell strikes nearby.

I watched in confusion. What was she doing?

The woman's eyes were wide open and intent, and just visible through the fog of her caul. There seemed to be purpose behind them, and when she stopped in the middle of the intersection and raised her hands high overhead, I suddenly realized she at least knew where she was. Physically, anyway, if not metaphysically. The psychotic and polychromatic images surely assaulting her since she rose after death were overpowering her clouded faculties.

If death wasn't enough, then afterlife would drive you mad. As was nearly the case with me, until Centurion Gustičić had found me.

And this woman, thinking herself still alive and walking Snipers' Alley in Sarajevo, was committing suicide — suicide Sarajevo-style. She was offering herself to the snipers in the mountains beyond the city. No one fired, of course, because people she could see and imagine could not see, let alone imagine, her. She was overcome with images of the past, present and future which assaulted her at once, and because she accepted them all as reality, she was *deranged*. All because a patrol had not found her. Until now.

I didn't know where my patrol was now. Perhaps they were diverted into the Oslobodjenje Building. If so, I'm thankful I did not join them, or else I'd never have saved this woman.

As I watched, though, my chance to save her was slipping away. While I stood in amazement watching her futilely offer herself to gunmen who could not kill her, a reaper launched himself toward the woman. Before I could shout a warning to him or cry in alarm to the woman, she was shackled and soon at his feet in manacles.

I stared, stupefied, then I finally challenged my enemy. "Reaper! Unhand her! She is under the protection of the Hierarchy."

Saint Vitus Dances Eternity

Žeteoc je podigao pogled brzo, oprezno. Bio je iznenadjen, ali nije izgledao uznemireno. To je bio krupan čovjek i njegovo izduženo, slavensko lice sa uvučenim očima i zategnutim obrazima bilo je pokriveno kovrčavom bradom, sličnom kakvu su nosili četnici. Odmah sam naježio.

"Sada!", viknuo sam dok sam iskoračavao iz ćoška. Moja pažnja je na trenutak prekinuta zbog tri iznenadna snajperska rafala dok je neki čovjek pretrčavao preko ulice. Snajperista, srećom, nije bio precizan.

Žeteoc se nagnuo i pritegnuo *okove* oko žene prije nego što je ponovo okrenuo glavu prema meni. Stajao je spreman ali nije izgledao napet ili nešto posebno pripremljen za akciju.

Smješkao se, brada mu se borala kao i ostatak njegovog lica. "Uštedićeš mi dugačak put, Legionaru, ukoliko se pobrineš za ovu ovdje."

Oklijevao sam zbog ovog čudnog odgovora, ali nisam propuštao trenutak i nepokolebljivo sam jurnuo prema Žeteocu. Kako sam se približavao, on je konačno shvatio da sam ja bio spreman za akciju i unervozio se.

"Šta to ti namjeravaš, Legionaru?"

Odlučno sam rekao: "Da spasim od tebe ovo jadno Dijete. Odmah je pusti na slobodu ili ću upotrijebiti silu. Moja patrola čeka nešto niže u Vojvode Putnika."

Žeteoc se povukao jedan korak unazad i pritegao stisak na lance: "Je li ovo neki trik?"

Ton njegova glasa je odavao nepovjerenje i *konfuziju*. Pitao sam se je li bilo ikakvoga načina da ovo iskoristim, ali ja sam bio isto tako zbunjen kao i on.

Jednostavno sam rekao: "Nije nikakav trik, Žeteoče. Ona nije tvoja da ti od nje profitiraš. Njena duša je da se spasi u Hijerarhiji."

Sada mu je bilo zabavno i naborao je lice. Lagano klimajući glavom Žeteoc je rekao: "Šta to, do vraga, govoriš? Sigurna??? Spašena? U Hijerarhiji? Je si li poludio?"

"Lud? Mahnit? Ne. Ljutit? Da."

The reaper looked up quickly, warily. He was surprised, but did not appear alarmed. He was a stout man, and his drawn, Slavic face with its sunken eyes and taut cheeks was mostly covered by a shaggy beard like the kind worn by the Četniks. I immediately bristled.

"Now!" I shouted as I strode from the corner. My attention was diverted for a moment by three rapid plinks of sniper fire as a man ran across the street. The sniper was, thankfully, not very good.

The reaper leaned over and tightened the *manacles* around the woman before straightening again to face me. He stood ready, but didn't appear tense or especially prepared for action.

He smiled, his beard wrinkling like the rest of his face. "You'll save me a long trip, Legionnaire, if you will take charge of this one."

I hesitated at this peculiar reply but did not relinquish my momentum and strode firmly toward the reaper. As I neared, he finally realized that I was ready for action and he tensed himself.

"Just what do you intend, Legionnaire?"

I said firmly, "To rescue this poor Enfant from you. Release her now or I will use force. My patrol is waiting just down Vojvode Putnika."

The reaper shuffled one foot backward and tightened his grip on the chains. "Is this a trick?"

His tone was one of incredulity, *confusion*. I wondered if there was any way I could take advantage of that, but I was just as confused as he was.

I simply said, "It's no trick, reaper. She is simply not yours to profit from. Her soul is to be safe within the Hierarchy."

It was now amusement that wrinkled his face. With a slight shake of his head, the reaper said, "What in the hell are you talking about? Safe? With the Hierarchy? Are you mad?"

"Mad? Crazy, no. Angry? Yes."

Sveti Vito Pleše za Vječnost

"Onda mora da si ti dio neke druge Hijerarhije," jednostavno je izustio, smeteno klimajući glavom.

Bio sam zbunjen kako je ovaj Srbin reagovao na moje zahtjeve da sam skoro zaboravio na okovano Dijete pri njegovim stopalima. Uzeo sam u obzir mogućnost da je ovaj Žeteoc u životu bio jedan od srpskih propagatora odgovornih za sramotne laži i *prevare* nacionalista.

Rekao sam odlučno, konačno: "Oslobodi je sada!"

"Ti si ili glup ili si zaludjen, "žestoko je uzvratio.

"Prokleti Žeteoče smrti!", zamahnuo sam da otrgnem njegovu ruku od okova koji su vezivali ženu. Samo što su moje ruke zafijukale precizno kroz zrak gdje je četnik bio, preplavilo me je iznenadno osjećanje vreline. Naglo sam sagnuo glavu ne znajući u potpunosti zašto. Bacajući letimičan pogled unazad, ugledao sam četnika koji se iznenada nekako našao iza mene, ispružen u zamahu gdje je bila moja glava. Reagovao sam dovoljno hitro da zamahnem svojom nogom unazad i da izbijem iz ravnoteže Žeteočevu drugu nogu. On se prevalio na tlo.

Dovršio sam praveći salto naprijed i stvorio nekoliko koraka distance. Svezano Dijete je sada bilo izmedju nas i svakog trena je trgalo lance. Bili su već zaključani.

"Ona je moj zatvorenik, Legionaru! Plati što će mi Hijerarhija dati u Lukavici ili jednostavno čekaj. Tvoja prokleta Hijerarhija će veoma brzo imati ovu *dušu*!"

Ne obazirući se na žeteočeve prijetnje, zgrabio sam okove žene u plazmatičnoj košuljici, te premjestio je iza sebe.

Žeteočevo lice je pocrvenilo od ljutine, "Vrlo dobro." Posegnuo je u tamne nabore njegove odjeće i izvukao dugački, zakrivljeni nož. Zavitlao je njime na mene. "Možda ćeš sada ponovo razmisliti."

Moje jedino oružje je bio mali relikvijski nož, za koji je Centurion Gustičić rekao da imam pravo nakon što sam izbavio prvo desetero Djece. Iako se činio maleckim i nekorisnim, izvukao sam bodež.

"Čuvaj se," upozorio sam ga, "ukoliko ne želiš da umreš. Dovoljno je da uzmeš ovo Dijete ali čekaj dok ostatak moje patrole čuje kako klevećeš trud Hijerarhije."

"You must be part of some other Hierarchy, then," he said flatly with a bewildered shake of his head.

I was so confused by how this Serb was reacting to my demands that I nearly forgot the manacled Enfant at his feet. I considered the possibility that this reaper was in life one of the Serb propagandists responsible for the outrageous lies and *deceits* of the nationalists.

I said firmly, finally, "Release her now!"

"You are either stupid or deluded," he spat.

"Damned reaper!" I lunged forward to rip his hands from the chains that bound the woman. Just as my hands swiped cleanly through the air where the Četnik had once been, a sudden feeling like a hot flash washed over me. I ducked without quite knowing why. Glancing back, I saw the Četnik, who was suddenly somehow behind me, extended in a kick at where my head had been. I reacted swiftly enough to kick one of my own legs backward and sweep the reaper's other foot from beneath him. He went sprawling to the ground.

I completed a forward somersault to put a couple paces of distance between us. The bound Enfant was now between us and I tugged at the chains momentarily. They were already locked.

"She is my prisoner, Legionnaire! Either pay what the Hierarchy will give me at Lukavica now, or simply wait. Your damned Hierarchy will have its *soul* soon enough!"

Heedless of the reaper's threat, I grabbed the chains around the cauled woman and repositioned her behind me.

The reaper's face shot crimson, "Very well." He reached into the dark folds of his clothing and withdrew a long, curved sword. He brandished it at me. "Perhaps now you'll reconsider."

My only weapon was a small relic knife that Centurion Gustičić said I was entitled to after I rescued my first ten Enfants. Though it seemed petite and ineffective, I drew the dagger.

"Hold your ground," I warned, "unless you wish to die. It's enough that you take this Enfant, but wait until the remainder of my patrol hears how you slander the work of the Hierarchy!"

Saint Vitus Dances Eternity

And this woman, thinking herself still alive and walking Snipers' Alley in Sarajevo, was committing suicide — suicide Sarajevo-style.

On se smijao. Ti si lud. Ili si i ti možda Dijete takodje, obmanjeno tim bezočnim lažima? Da je samo bilo tako jednostavno prevariti Sarajlije u životu! Tako jednostavno kao što je varati ignorantne vodje zapadnih zemalja!"

Kako sam ga mrzio! Jer je bio srpski četnik. Jer je bio Žeteoc, žeteoc smrti. On je bio sve ono čemu sam se ja suprotstavljao u obadva životna vijeka. Želio sam da rastrgnem njegov plazmatični kostur ali nešto od onoga što je rekao nije zvučalo lažno. Imao sam neočekivani osjećaj da je ovaj mrtvi čovjek bio nekako važan za mene. Je li se to moglo vidjeti u drugima? Kako konvencioňalno - kako čudesno - kao da su se oni koji su mogli oblikovati moju *sudbinu* uvijek isticali takvim nepogrešivim uvidima!

Rekoh: "Neću popustiti, ali saslušaću tvoje laži još za trenutak prije nego što pozovem patrolu. Pa reci mi sada zašto sam lud!"

Žeteoc se odmaknuo korak nazad dok je polagano spuštao i odlagao nož. Pažljivo me je gledao i rekao povjerljivo: "Pretpostavljam da si sam, Legionaru. Prvo, da si dio obližnje patrole, onda bi neko od njih već stigao ovdje, ili bi ih ti odmah pozvao. Drugo, ne mogu da vjerujem da si ravnopravan član Hijerarhije ako vjeruješ u te laži što si mi napričao. Zbog toga.... ja sam taj koji kontroliše situaciju." To posljednje je naglasio odlučnim zamahom ukošene ruke.

Nastavio je dok sam ja samo zurio u njega. "Reci mi ovo, Legionaru: Šta će se dogoditi ovoj ženi ako je ja zaista prepustim u tvoj nadzor?"

"Ona će biti isporučena do Centuriona, koji će je predati zajedno sa svim drugima koje smo ovoga dana spasili od takvih kao što si ti, od Otpadnika ili od besciljnog, konfuznog bivstvovanja poput njenog." Pokazao sam na ženu. Ona je drhturila u željeznim karikama.

"Da. A šta je sa njenom sudbinom poslije toga?"

"Ona će biti premještena iz ovog grada razorenog paklom i poslana u Stygiju da postane stanovnik grada mrtvih."

Žeteoc je odmahnuo glavom i rekao: "Pogrešno."

"Pa reci mi ti, Žeteoče. Šta je njena sudbina kada je u rukama Hijerhahije? Pomenuo si da ćeš je prodati Hijerarhiji. Da je tako, možda si ti manje vrijedan osude nego oni Žeteoci koji bi je prodali u *roblje*, ali kakva god da je sudbina očekuje u Hijerarhiji, sigurno da nije gora od izručenja koje bi ti napravio."

He laughed, "You are mad! Are you but an Enfant too to be beguiled by such shameful lies? If only Sarajevans in life had been so easy to fool! As easy as the ignorant leaders of the western nations!"

How I hated him! For being a Četnik Serb. For being a reaper. He was all I'd opposed in two lifetimes. I wanted to sunder his plasmic frame, but something of what he said didn't sound false. I had a sudden sense that this dead man was somehow important to me. Could one see that in others? How convenient — how wonderful — if those who might shape my *destiny* always shone with such unmistakable light!

I said, "I won't yield, but I will listen to your lies for a moment more before calling my patrol. So tell me why I'm mad!"

The reaper stepped back a pace as he languidly dipped and glided his sword. He looked at me closely and said conspiratorially, "I suspect you are alone, Legionnaire. First, if you were part of a nearby patrol, then more of them would have arrived by now, or you would have called for them immediately. Secondly, I cannot believe that you are even a member of the Hierarchy if you believe the kinds of lies you've told me. Therefore, it is I... who control this situation." The last he said with a final flourish of his sword.

He continued when I only glared at him, "Tell me this, Legionnaire: What is it that would happen to this woman if I did release her to your custody?"

"She would be delivered to my Centurion, who would deliver her with any others we've saved this day from the likes of you and the Renegades or an aimless, confused existence like this one's." I pointed to the woman. She trembled within the links of steel.

"Yes. And what of her fate after that?"

"She would be transferred from this hell-torn city and sent to Stygia to become a citizen of the city of the dead."

The reaper shook his head and said, "Wrong."

"Then tell me, reaper. What is her fate when in the hands of the Hierarchy? You mention selling her to the Hierarchy. If so, then perhaps you are less reprehensible than the reapers who will sell her into *slavery*; but surely whatever fate holds for her with the Hierarchy is no worse than the consignment you would make."

Saint Vitus Dances Eternity

"To je isto, budalo!" Žeteočev nož je zaparao zrak u razočarenju.

"Nisi nikada dosada bio u Stygiji, zar ne?" Odmahnuo sam glavom.

"Onda možda zaista ne znaš da ti sakupljaš Duše koje postaju igračke poglavara Stygije i njihovih omiljenih udvorica. Zar ne shvataš da će ova žena biti predata u ruke pronalazača koji će je potpuno preoblikovati u neku vrstu relikvije, možda baš kao taj bodež što tako silovito stišćeš? Ili, ako je slaba i bezvrijedna, njena duša može postati samo jedan novčić, što se može iskoristiti da se pribave drugi predmeti i usluge medju mrtvima?"

"Lažeš."

"Ne, i to je zbog čega sam ja Žeteoc, Legionaru. Stygijini gospodari moga života, Milošević i Karadžić, poslali su me u *grob*. Zašto bih, ponovo ovdje, borio se za njima slične? Ili zašto se pridružiti drugoj blesavoj grupi kao što su Lazareni - koji su istinski razlog pokolja ovdje, čak iako je Hijerarhija ta što smanjuje krvoprolića."

Nisam mogao, nisam želio to prihvatiti. "Dokaži."

Žeteoc se nasmijao. "Ne mislim da imaš snage za istinu."

"Imao sam snage da se suočim sa lažima što su mi govorili ljudi slični tebi, četniče. Mogu se suočiti i sa lažima koje mi ti sada govoriš."

Nasmijao se ponovo. Nimalo ne razljućen političkim žaokama. "Vrlo dobro."

Razmišljao je za trenutak, onda se opustio i rekao, "Vodi ovu ženu tvom Centurionu. Večeras, kada je predaš kao što ti kažeš, pod zaštitu i nadzor Hijerarhije, posjetićemo je u Lukavici. Srešćemo se ponovo ovdje u *ponoć*. Ona neće biti transportovana izvan grada sve do kasno naveče."

"Šta je cijena toga? Zašto je predaješ meni?"

"Jednostavno. Kada vidiš da sam u pravu, dugovaćeš mi novčić."

"A šta onda ako sam ja onaj koji je u pravu?"

"Ti ćeš već dobiti svoju nagradu," rekao je, upućujući na ženu koja je sada bila potpuno prikovana za zemlju pod težinom lanaca.

"Istina," potvrdio sam. "Vrlo dobro, prihvatam. Sada je oslobodi."

"It's the same, fool!" The reaper's sword slashed the air in frustration. "You've never been to Stygia, have you?"

I shook my head.

"Then perhaps you truly don't understand that you are collecting the souls that become the playthings of the Stygian lords and their favored minions. Don't you realize that this woman will be put in the hands of an artificer who will mold her entirely into a relic of some sort, perhaps like that dagger you clench so furiously? Or, if she is weak and worthless, her soul may become a single coin, a single obulus which can be used to purchase other items and services among the dead?"

"You're lying."

"No, and that's why I reap, Legionnaire. The Stygian lords of my life, Milošević and Karadžić, sent me to my *grave*. Why, once here, would I fight for their likes again? Or why join another crazy group like the Lazarians — who are the true cause of the slaughter here, even if it is the Hierarchy that feeds off the carnage."

I couldn't, wouldn't, accept it. "Prove it."

The reaper laughed. "I don't think you have the stomach for the truth."

"I had the strength to face the lies your kind told me in life, Četnik. I can face the lies you tell now."

He laughed again, not angered at all by the political barbs. "Very well."

He thought for a moment, then relaxed and said, "Take this woman to your Centurion. Tonight, after she is turned over, as you say, to the protective custody of the Hierarchy, we will visit her at Lukavica. We will meet again here at *midnight*. She will not be transported out of the city until later tonight."

"What's the price? Why release her to me?"

"Simple. When you see that I am right, you will owe an obulus."

I said, "And when it is I am who am correct?"

"You will already have your prize," he said, motioning to the woman who was now entirely on the ground under the weight of the chains.

"True," I admitted. "Very well, I accept. Now release her."

Sveti Vito Pleše za Vječnost

As he resheathed his curved *sword*, he presented a pair of keys with his other hand and calmly unfastened the locks.

I knelt by the woman, trying to assure her that everything was okay. When I stood, I helped her rise beside me. I was relieved with my victory, but the reaper had planted a seed of doubt.

I said, "Here, at midnight."

"Yes."

With that I wandered away and maneuvered the woman out of the paths of the people still racing to avoid sniper fire.

The reaper shouted one last command to me as I steadied the staggering Enfant. "Remember, Legionnaire, to wear no emblems of your office."

Which meant I must leave my dagger. That's when I knew for certain he was lying, but I would go along with his game.

...

I returned at midnight after placing the woman in the charge of Centurion Gustičić and learning that the patrol had indeed been reassigned to watch for *casualties* near the Oslobodjenje Building.

I saw the reaper was waiting for me. "How do you propose we get to Lukavica? It's miles from here."

"Easy, Legionnaire. We hitch a ride. Let's go to the Holiday Inn."

He started to move, then stopped and turned. "By the way," he asked, "what's your name?"

"Dragoš." I made no reciprocal inquiry.

"Serb too, eh?"

"No, Bosnian."

The reaper smiled. "Right."

Saint Vitus Dances Eternity

I recalled a conversation I'd had in life with another surgeon about the snipers here.

Za kratko smo stigli do Holidej Inna. Ovaj hotel je bio posljednji koji je još radio u Sarajevu. Sada je služio kao dom desetinama stranih novinara, medju njima možda nekoliko zapadnjaka koji su shvatali raspon ove tragedije.

Bilo je uznemiravajuće prelaziti hotelski trg da bi se prišlo zgradi. Iako su ovo bili rani jutarnji sati, znao sam da snajperisti još uvijek posmatraju. Čekajuci na neku osobu uspavanu tim sitnim satima.

Sjetio sam se razgovora o snajperistima, što sam imao sa drugim hirurgom, u životu. Taj hirurg je tvrdio da je raspoznavao djelovanje odredjenih snajperista. Kada bi doznao iz kojeg dijela grada je bila žrtva, mogao je pogoditi vrstu rane prije nego što bi se suočio sa žrtvom. Radnik u fabrici na Bistriku po povratku sa smjene? U tom slučaju uzmi dvije dodatne boce krvi jer je to pogodatak u crijevo. Neko je pogodjen na hotelskom trgu pored Holidej Inna usred noći? Onda se pripremi da *amputiraš*, jer su kosti desne noge razmrskane sa tri hica. Sa Baščaršije u Starom Gradu? Onda se spremi na umotavanje leša. Žrtva je sigurno usmrćena preciznim pogotkom u glavu nešto iznad lijevog uha.

Kako je on to znao? I kako je znao da je posljednja zrtva bila žena? Slušao sam sumnjičavo kad mi je rekao da neki od snajperista očigledno umišljalju da su umjetnici. Oni potpisuju svoj rad stvarajući karakterističnu ranu, kao hirurzi koji prave karakteristične ureze da bi obilježili svoj rad. Ne samo da snajperisti pucaju samo na odredjenim lokacijama nego ponekad imaju specijalne mete takodje. Ne samo "isključivo žene" nego, ponekad, i "isključivo djeca."

Ali bili smo nevidljivi za *snajperistu* koji je ciljao na noge i ležernim korakom smo stigli do ulaznih hotelskih vrata, što nijedan živi čovjek ne bi mogao sebi dozvoliti.

Žeteoc je rekao: "Hajde da sačekamo i vidimo hoće li neko otvoriti vrata. Vozila UNPROFOR-a se neće povući još za narednih pola sata."

Mogli smo proći kroz vrata ali to je boljelo. Nakon nekoliko trenutaka tihe ćutnje, bez bilo koga ko se zadržavao ispred vrata ili namjeravao da ih upotrijebi, morali smo da izdržimo kratki ubod bola što se radjao narušavanjem fizičkih granica svijeta živih.

It didn't take long to walk to the Holiday Inn. The hotel was the last one operating in Sarajevo. It now served as the home to dozens of foreign journalists, among them perhaps the only Westerners to understand the scope of the tragedy here.

It was nerve-wracking to cross the hotel plaza to reach the building. Though it was the early hours of the morning, I knew that snipers were still watching. Waiting for a person lulled to sleep by the hour of night.

I recalled a conversation I'd had in life with another surgeon about the snipers here. The surgeon claimed he recognized the work of certain snipers. When he learned what area of the city a victim was from, he could guess the wound before even confronted with the victim. A factory worker from the Bistrik District as shifts changed? Then get two extra pints of blood because it's a gut shot. Shot in the hotel plaza at the Holiday Inn in the middle of the night? Then prepare to *amputate* because the bones of the right leg have been shattered by three shots. From Baščaršija in Old Town? Then pack up. She's already dead from a shot clean through the head just above the left ear.

How did he know? And how could he know that last one was definitely a woman? I listened incredulously as he told me that some of these snipers apparently fancied themselves artists. They signed their work with signature wound, like surgeons who make characteristic incisions to mark their work. Not only do they shoot only certain locations, but sometimes only specific targets as well. Not just "only women," but sometimes "only children" too.

But we were invisible to the *sniper* who aimed for legs, and reached the front doors of the hotel at a leisurely pace that no one living could afford.

The reaper said, "Let's wait to see if someone will open the door. The UNPROFOR vehicles aren't scheduled to pull out for another half hour."

We could step through the doors, but that would hurt. After several moments of silent waiting, and without anyone even lingering near the doors or threatening their use, we had to endure the brief stab of pain that came with breaking the physical laws of the living world.

Saint Vitus Dances Eternity

As we entered the lobby I noted a number of signs that indicated changes to the operation of the hotel because of the siege. The only one I took the time to read notified diners that meals were served in the old conference room because the dining room had a wall of windows facing the hills to the south of the city, and people in the room were therefore at risk. It didn't specifically spell out the *danger*, which was snipers with telescopic sights who could shoot a tine off a fork in a diner's hand if they wished.

Of course, that entire side of the Holiday Inn was nearly obliterated now.

I followed the reaper past the check-in and reservations desks. This area of the hotel seemed just like any I'd ever seen. The clerk on duty seemed perfectly alert, unafraid, and absolutely unaware that she was inside a crumbling building within a dying city under siege.

I tried to ignore this and followed the reaper to an elevator that led to the underground garage. The reaper tried to exchange words with me twice while we waited, but the clerk was still on my mind.

She surely had wonderful opportunities to remind Foreign Ministers and diplomats and UNPROFOR representatives that they visited a slowly dying city as she checked them in and out. Did she at least mutter a word in favor of succor for the 400,000 civilians within the city? Or would that be unprofessional and disrupt the officials' pleasant visit with a jolt of reality?

"You are a thoughtful one," the reaper said, finally piercing my haze of concentration.

"I suppose."

"Wondering if I am, after all, correct?"

I said, "That doesn't worry me. You're wrong."

"Then why are you coming?"

"Because it was the *price* of your releasing the woman to my care."

The reaper shook his head and, for the first time, stroked his beard. "If that's the only reason you're coming, then forget it." He waved his hand. "And you claim the West is close-minded!"

Sveti Vito Pleše za Vječnost

He continued somberly, "I waive the price. Have the woman with my prayers for you both." He looked at me earnestly and almost repeated, "For both your souls." Then he began to walk away.

At first I was startled, then relieved, then I wanted to call after him, to tell him that there was another reason — I needed to know without doubt that I was right. I could no longer simply accept old beliefs as fact. Not in light of the truths that surrounded me every moment: ethnic cleansing, *genocide*, and wholesale destruction. And certainly not in light of what might be truth: a five hundred year battle between the ghosts of a Serbian and an Ottoman warrior and a Hierarchy that was perhaps everything I despised.

Nothing would surprise me now.

I still didn't call to the reaper.

Nor did I leave after him.

I waited patiently by the elevator. Perhaps there were stairs somewhere. Then I realized that elevators wouldn't be the same as passing through a glass door. While they would seem more complicated for a ghost, they were actually far simpler. All I needed was to embody myself just enough to exert a little pressure on the buttons.

I concentrated and then pushed the down button. Within moments the elevator *dinged*, and one of the doors opened. I noted with some satisfaction that the clerk at least noticed this unexplained arrival and departure of a elevator car. Perhaps she was aware of her surroundings after all.

Soon the doors closed and the elevator hesitated. I embodied myself briefly again and pushed the button marked "Parking." The elevator shuddered and then rumbled down. It opened to reveal a garage full of the largest collection of battered and beaten cars I have ever seen. Many of them were lettered with *graffiti*, but all of them sported the wounds of shells and snipers. In a glance I took in a wobbly-tired Russian jeep, some sort of Renault with doors that looked glued on and a battered car of unrecognizable make that had a message written on both the hood and trunk that read in English complete with the misspelling, "Don't shoot, don't waste your bullet. I am immortel".

I didn't spot an intact front windshield anywhere in the garage.

Saint Vitus Dances Eternity

Sve dok nisam spazio kratku kolonu koju su sačinjavala tri UNPROFOR-ova blindirana vozila. Bili su to Panhardi za izvidjanje. Bijeli sa zatamnjenim zračnim puškarnicama sa strane. Dvosjedi, ali se samo pet ljudi motalo oko njih. Možda sam se mogao smjestiti na sjedište, umjesto da se krijem medju opremom koju su nosili.

Sva petorica su imali radne uniforme i beretke. Izgledali su kao zapadni Evropljani. Dok je jedan od njih pričao, govoreći nešto o vremenu što nisam mogao potpuno razumjeti, shvatio sam da su bili Francuzi. Francuzi su bili medju onima koji su bili dosta posvećeni bosanskom *ratu*, sudeći bar po broju "čuvara mira."

Trebao mi je samo tren da shvatim da će suvozačeva strana biti zaključana, tako da sam odlučio da se provučem unutra kroz vozačeva vrata. Izgledalo je da srednji Panhard nosi najmanje stvari, pa sam se popeo u njega i pribio se uz stražnji dio.

Jedan oficir se ubrzo približio petorici Francuza i onda su se oni odmah razmiljeli prema vozilima i uspeli se unutra. Vožnja prema Lukavici je počela.

Posmatrao sam kroz prorez na vjetrobranu, dok smo se punom brzinom kretali prema rampi u garaži, prateći Panhard koji je išao naprijed, i nastavljajući po planu ka Snajperskoj aleji i konačno, prema Lukavici. Tmina i moj zgrčeni položaj su činili nemogućim da vidim bilo što za vrijeme vožnje. Na sreću.

Iskoristio sam ovaj trenutak relativne sigurnosti da se okrijepim dok sam očekivao da ugledam Lukavicu. Čuo sam od drugoga Legionara, koji je još uvijek provjeravao šta mu je sa porodicom u Sarajevu, da je oko dvije hiljade ljudi bilo deportovano do *baraka* u Lukavici, samo tri ili četiri dana ranije. To su bili civili - koji su odvedeni kao ratni zarobljenici direktno iz njihovih stanova bliže paklu sotone Karadžića.

Nakon što se Panhard otkotrljao do stajališta, na osvijetljeno zemljište oko predjašnjih baraka, gdje je sada bio koncentracioni logor, izvukao sam se kroz suvozačeva vrata. Nisam tačno znao gdje da idem. Za trenutak sam posmatrao naokolo, i vidio sam ono što je Žeteoc najvjerovatnije namjeravao da mi pokaže. Tamo gdje su se završavale zgrade, nalazilo se odjeljenje tako ruševno i istrulo da sam čak i ja osjećao jezu. To je mjesto zasigurno bilo posjećivano duhovima. I svakako to je bilo područje gdje nijedan smrtnik ne bi došao blizu. Bila je to očito kuća duhova.

Dok sam se približavao, primjetio sam dva Legionara na straži. Pitam se kakvu je varku Žeteoc smislio da bi prošao pored njih. Je li ovo uostalom bilo pravo mjesto?

Until I noted the short line of three UNPROFOR armored cars. They were all Panhard scouts. They were all white with darkened air vents lining the sides. Only two-seaters, but I saw just five people lingering near them. Perhaps I'd have a seat to myself instead of hiding among the equipment they carried.

All five of the men were dressed in fatigues and berets. They looked Western European. When one spoke, saying something about the time that I couldn't fully understand, I realized they were French. The French were among the Europeans more dedicated to the Bosnian *war*, though only if you judged by numbers of "peacekeepers."

It took a moment for me to realize that the passenger side of each car would probably be locked, so I decided to slip in through the driver's door instead. The middle Panhard seemed to carry the fewest goods, so I climbed in and pressed myself toward the rear.

The five Frenchmen were soon joined by an officer, and they all immediately dispersed to their vehicles and clambered in. The drive to Lukavica began.

I watched through the slitted windshield as we raced up the ramp of the parking garage, following the Panhard in front, and pursued a course down Snipers' Alley and eventually toward Lukavica. The darkness and my cramped conditions made it almost impossible to see anything during the trip. Fortunately.

I took this moment of relative safety to refresh myself as I prepared to face Lukavica. I'd heard from another Legionnaire who still checked on his Sarajevan family that, only three or four days ago, about 2000 people were deported to the *barracks* at Lukavica. These were civilian prisoners of war taken directly from their apartments straight to a hell closer to the devil Karadžić.

After the Panhard rolled to a stop within the brightly lit grounds around the former barracks, now a concentration camp, I wrestled out of the passenger door. I didn't know where exactly to go. But, after looking around for a moment, I saw what the reaper probably intended to show me. At the far end of the building was a section so dilapidated and rotten that even I felt a chilly emanation. It was definitely haunted. Certainly an area that no mortal would stray near. Clearly, it was the home of ghosts.

As I neared it, I noted there were two Legionnaires on guard. I wondered what ploy the reaper planned to get past them. Was this even the right place?

Sveti Vito Pleše za Vječnost

I knew it had to be. But could I get in without lying to the guards? I could think of nothing. Nor could I think of a suitable lie since I didn't know what was inside. Was I ready to risk my position in the patrol over a foolish, niggling question? I knew at once I was. If my new *suspicions* were incorrect, then the Hierarchy would prove to be the kind of organization that would forgive me for such a transgression. If, on the other hand, the reaper was right, then my status be damned.

I backed up so I could approach the guards within full sight for a good distance. I immediately drew their attention.

"Good evening," I said as I drew near them.

They remained expressionless, so I pressed, "I need to check inside for a relic of Centurion Gustičić. He lost it here earlier and claims he looked everywhere else. So, he sent me."

They didn't budge, so I rattled on, running my lie into the ground. I wished I had my dagger so I had some proof of my station.

"I'm just a grunt, so I was chosen to come all the way back out here. Just let me have a look, will you, please?"

"Sure," one of them said finally.

"Great," I said before I could think of how *foolish* it sounded.

Each of the guards drew a key from within their drab grey fatigues and simultaneously unlocked nearly identical padlocks on the bars blocking the doors.

The other said, "Just hurry, or we'll lock you in with them. They might take you by accident too."

A chill rang my spine dry. Suddenly I didn't want to enter.

"Hurry," the second guard repeated more urgently.

I stumbled forward into the darkness. All I saw at first was that a light source, a fire, burned in the rear of the room. It grew larger and brighter when the doors swung nearly shut behind me.

The contorted faces emerged from the darkness like bloated and pasty corpses bobbing to the surface of an inky sea.

A tada su jauci doprijeli do mojih ušiju. To je bio žagor prokletih, a ne spašenih duša. Plamen relikvijske baklje u pozadini sobe polako je osvijetljavao lica desetina Djece koja su se gurala u sobi. Svjetlo je zahvatalo i polako otkrivalo njihova blijeda lica. Izobličena lica koja su se pojavljivala iz tame kao naduvani i ljepljivi leševi što su se klatili na površini zacrnjenoga mora. Pošto su im glave bile nepokrivene, mogao sam vidjeti da je većina duhova još uvijek nosila plazmične košuljice.

Moje misli su se kovitlale u konfuziji. Moje plazmatično srce je otkucavalo u strepnji. Razmišljao sam - ne, nadao sam se - da postoji odgovor na sve ovo dok sam mahnito trčao tražeći bilo kakav dokaz da ovo nije bila istina.

Nasao sam *dokaz*. Ali bio je nepovoljan, i to onaj koji se ne zaboravlja. Žena iz Snajperske aleje ležala je srušena izmedju dvije druge žene, neke starije gospodje koja je ubijena snajperskim hicem, i djevojke koja je još uvijek nosila tragove šrapnelskih krhotina što su je razderale na komade.

Žena koju sam izvukao iz okova i izručio Centurionu Gustičiću kao dušu što treba biti oslobodjena je, umjesto toga, bila ovdje! Ponovo zatočena. Zgurana kao neki predmet, nečije vlasništvo, u ovu malu odaju. Kao tele u mraku štale. Još uvijek je nosila svoju plazmatičnu košuljicu i njene oči su bile iskolačene od straha, što mi je dovoljno govorilo.

Proveo sam mjesece boreći se ne za one koji su bili sablasni duplikat Plavih šljemova, nego za one koji su bili kao Četnici? *Odvratno*. I dok sam razmišljao o tome, opet, moje staro poredjenje Plavih šljemova sa Hijerarhijom je postajalo sve prikladnije.

Stresao sam se.

Vrata su zaškripala otvarajući se. "Požuri."

Gotovo sam zavrištao kad je to neznatno otvaranje vrata bacilo dovoljno dodatnog svjetla u sobu pa sam vidio bebe. I one su bile takodje u okovima. Jednoj su nedostajale obadvije noge što znači da je vjerovatno bila ubijena ležeći, u bolnici; nakon što je jedva preživjela prva granatiranja. Prema svima se ophodilo sa istim stupnjem nemilosti i nepoštovanja - nevine duše vezane za svaku vrstu pakla što sam mogao zamisliti.

Pokušao sam da smislim šta bih mogao uraditi. Katanci na ovim lancima su bili mnogo manji nego oni na vratima. Nije bilo nikakve šanse da ključevi, što su stražari posjedovali, mogu otvoriti bilo koju od ovih brava.

Then the moans reached my ears. It was the murmur of damned, not rescued, souls. The flame of the relic torch at the back of the room slowly illuminated the faces of dozens of Enfants crowded into the room. The light caught and slowly revealed their pale faces. The contorted faces emerged from the darkness like bloated and pasty corpses bobbing to the surface of an inky sea. As the heads were unveiled, I could see that most of the ghosts still wore their cauls.

My mind leaped in confusion. My plasmic heart beat with alarm. I wondered — no, I hoped — that there was an explanation for it all as I ran the aisles frantically looking for something to prove that this was not what it seemed.

I found the *proof*. But it was damning, unforgiving. The woman from Snipers' Alley lay crushed between two other women, one an elderly lady killed by a sniper, and the other an adolescent still bearing the marks of the shrapnel fragments that tore her to pieces.

The woman I'd unchained and delivered to Centurion Gustičić as a soul about to be freed was here instead! Chained again. Crowded like a thing, a possession, into this small chamber. Like a veal calf in a dark barn. She still wore her caul, and her eyes were large with a fear that sang to me.

I'd spent months fighting not for the ghostly counterpart of the Blue Helmets, but for those like the Četniks? *Abominable*. As I thought about it, though, my old Blue Helmet-Hierarchy comparison became even more apt.

I trembled.

A door creaked open. "Hurry."

I almost cried out when that slight opening spilled enough additional light into the room for me to see the babies. They too were chained. One was missing both legs, which means he was probably killed while lying in the hospital after already barely surviving a first shelling. All were treated with equal degrees of disgrace and irreverence — innocent souls bound for every kind of hell I could imagine.

I tried to think what I might do. The padlocks on these chains were far smaller than the large ones on the door. There was absolutely no chance that the keys the guards possessed would open any of these locks.

Saint Vitus Dances Eternity

The pavement rippled like an ocean, lifting the children into a gout of flame and concussion that blew them like weightless angels, tattered T-shirts whipping behind them like the stumps of wings.

Bacio sam posljednji pogled na ove proklete duše. Ovdje bih i ja mogao ostati, zbog moje budalaste *lakovjernosti*.

Posrtao sam, još uvijek drhteći. Ovaj put sam hodao miljama nazad prema središtu Sarajeva.

…

Samo sam želio da pustim mrtve da biju svoje vlastite bitke. Naposlijetku, njihovi sukobi bili su zasnovani na vijekovnim raspravama koje ja nisam mogao dokučiti. Ili je možda to jedna jedina rasprava koja traje šest stotina godina. Jesu li ratovi na Balkanu bili samo nastavak zavade Murata Prvoga i Lazara? Ako se njihovo *neprijateljstvo* prelijevalo na svijet živih, kao što sam sumnjao da jeste, opiranje nije bilo moguće jer nikakav napredak nije bio vjerovatan.

Ukoliko je moć osjećaja srž onoga što duh postane kada se umre, onda su duhovi Sarajeva imali neku vrstu metafizičke predodredjenosti da vode borbu koja se nikad ne završava - borbu koja se poslije smrti roditelja nastavlja u životu djece.

To su bila moja razmišljanja dva dana kasnije. Nisam se prijavio na zadatak u patroli i doznao sam da me je Centurion Gustičić, koji je za mnom tragao, smatrao dezerterom.

Sjeo sam pribivši se uz srušenu kuću i osluškivao granate koje su nastavljale da padaju na grad. Tutnjalo je u pozadini. Djeca, koju sam vidio da se igraju u ovoj ulici poškropljenoj snijegom usitnjenog stakla, nisu se trzala na odjeke eksplozije. To je sve bilo sada dio njihovog svijeta i oni su se navikli. Nastavili su se igrati. Nogometna lopta je odskakala izmedju njih kao vrući krompir, ili kao prava bomba

I ja sam, takodje, mogao priznati svoj svijet, ali se nisam još uvijek privikao.

I konačno sam shvatio da nisam bio u pravu.

U toku mog bijega od prije dva dana, posmatrao sam kako Plavac uzima stotinu njemačkih maraka od Sarajlije u zamjenu za transport izvan grada. To je bio drugi Sarajlija koji će živjeti. I jedan od rijetkih koji su možda mogli vjerovati da su Plavi šljemovi bili heroji. Jedan od rijetkih koji su mogli vjerovati da je vanjski svijet izvan ovog paklenog igrališta čak mogao stvarati heroje. Ali svijetu treba više od heroja. Jednostavna volja da odbiješ izdati svoju savjest čini te herojem.

I swept a last look at the damned souls. But for my foolish *gullibility*, here too would go I.

I stumbled out, still trembling. This time I walked the miles back to the heart of Sarajevo.

…

I just wanted to let the dead fight their own battles. After all, their conflicts were grounded in centuries-old disputes I could not fathom anyway. Or perhaps a single 600-year-old dispute. Were the wars through the ages in the Balkans just a continuation of the feud between Murat I and Lazar? If their *hatred* was spilling over into the world of the living, as I suspected it was, then resistance was impossible because success was implausible.

If the essence of what a ghost becomes is the puissance of its emotions as it dies, then the ghosts of Sarajevo had a sort of metaphysical predisposition to fight an unending battle — a battle that goes beyond death for the parents and continues in life for the children.

Such were my ruminations two days later. I'd not reported to my patrol assignment and had learned that Centurion Gustičić, who was tracking me, considered me AWOL.

I sat pressed against a crumbling home listening as shells continued to fall upon the city. It was only so much background noise now. Children I saw playing on this street sprinkled in a snow of powdered glass did not even flinch at the reverberations of the blasts. This was a part of their world now, and they'd adapted. They kept on playing. The soccer ball bouncing among them like a hot potato, or a live bomb.

Though I too could acknowledge my world, I still hadn't adapted.

But I did finally realize that I was wrong.

During my flight of the last two days, I once watched as a Blue Helmet accepted a hundred Deutsch Marks from a Sarajevan in return for transport out of the city. It was another Sarajevan who would live. And one of the few who could perhaps believe that the Blue Helmets were heroes. One who could believe that the world outside this hellish playground could even produce heroes. But heroes aren't enough for the world anymore. The simple will to resist betraying your conscience makes you a hero.

Saint Vitus Dances Eternity

I smiled at her as I lifted the boy to my chest where I closely hugged his shivering body.

Gdje je to mene vodilo?

Ako samo razumijevanje da sam pravio iste greške kao i ostatak čovječanstva, te odbijanje da nastavim sa greškama, je to što me čini herojem, onda su heroji prokleti. Sve što se o meni time kaže je, da sam, u najmanju ruku, prošao osnovni ispit iz humanosti.

Svijet je pogrešno razmišljao o Bosni - da je rat bio *izvan domašaja* jer je navodno, bio zasnovan u nacionalnoj mržnji što traje vijekovima. To nije bilo tako. Ovaj rat je bio igra snaga u šačici izdajničkih ludjaka koji su stvorili saučesnike u srpskome narodu i sada na njih prebacivali da završe što je započeto.

U ovom dijelu bijega, odlučio sam da formiram grupu pravih spasioca za mrtve u Sarajevu. Nova patrola da obavlja zadatke što sam mislio da sam ja odista obavljao u Hijerarhiji. Konačno možda bih mogao potpuno zaustaviti transport sarajevskih duša u Stygiju. A nije li to bilo isto tako ograničeno kao i ono što su predstavljali Plavi šljemovi? Zalog u reakciji na veće zlo? Herojski zadatak?

Da, ali to bi bio *početak* samo. Istina, morao bih da se borim protiv Hijerarhije čak i poslije vremena kada njihova trgovina u Sarajevu bude prestala. To bi značilo postati najboljim primjerom za sve podjarmljene ljude - nekom vrstom sveca.

Biti svetac je značilo utjeloviti vrline heroja ali djelovati sa većom pronicljivošću. To je značilo imati veliki osjećaj za pravdu koji se ne prezasićuje trenutnim herojskim akcijama. To je značilo biti heroj čak i onda kada heroji nisu u potražnji. To je takodje značilo da je čovjek možda suviše mali da djeluje protiv nečega što je veliko. Kao što sam ja, bez sumnje, bio u očima Hijerarhije.

Ali to je prvo značilo da si požrtvovan.

Sada sam shvatio zašto su drugi prije mene smatrali da je lakše biti heroj nego svetac. Jer se svijet odazivao samo na heroje, i brza rješenja. Kada je nezadovoljstvo svecima svugdje tako veliko, šta više da čovjek uradi? Šta manje?

Koračao sam prema djeci nadajući se da ću i ja, takodje, naći odgovor u njihovoj raznolikosti. Tajnu koja im je omogućila da se ne obaziru na razaranje oko njih pa se još uvijek pretvaraju da su djeca.

Where did that leave me?

If merely comprehending that I was making the same mistakes as the rest of humanity and resisting perpetuating the mistakes makes me a hero, then heroes be damned. All that says about me is that I have at least passed a basic test of humanity.

For the world thought wrongly of Bosnia — that the war was *unfathomable* because it was supposedly rooted in centuries of ethnic hatred. It wasn't. This war was the powerplay of a handful of traitorous madmen who created accomplices in the Serbian people and now guilted them all into completing what had been started.

In this time of flight I decided I would forge a group of true saviors for the dead of Sarajevo. A new patrol to do the job I thought I'd done with the Hierarchy. Eventually I might halt the transport of Sarajevans souls to Stygia completely. But was that as small-minded as what the Blue Helmets represented? A token response to greater ills? A hero's task?

Yes, but it would be only a *beginning*. To be true I would have to fight the Hierarchy even beyond the time when their traffic in Sarajevo had ended. It would mean becoming the standard-bearer for all subjected people — a saint of sorts.

To be a saint meant to embody the virtues of the hero but to act with greater vision. It meant knowing a sense of injustice too large to be sated by momentary heroic action. It meant being a hero even when heroes weren't in demand. It also meant knowing that you might be too small to make a difference against something so large. Like I undoubtedly was in the face of the Hierarchy.

But first it meant to care at all.

Then I realized why others before me found it easier to be a hero than a saint. Because the world only responded to heroes, the quick fix. When ennui everywhere is too great for saints, what more could one person do? What less?

I walked toward the children, hoping that in their diversion I too would find an answer. The secret that allowed them to ignore the destruction around them and still at least pretend to be children.

Saint Vitus Dances Eternity

Iznenada, medju njima, osjetio sam se nevidljivim kao što sam uistinu bio. Čak i da me smrt nije dijelila od njih, ne bi me vidjeli jer su njihove sjajne oči pratile bijelu loptu što se vrtila. Njihova tijela su se uvijala i skakutala, a njihovi udovi pomamno mahali i živahno *plesali*, očekujući i slijedeći loptu. Za njih, u ovom trenutku, nijedan drugi svijet nije postojao.

Ali kao što je bilo mjesecima, ovaj svijet je prodirao u njihovu uobrazilju. Poput lopte što skakuće prema glavi male, energične djevojčice, tako je munjevito projurila neka sjenka.

Nijedna grmljavina u prirodi se ne bi mogla oglasiti takvom snagom kao bomba što je zatresla zemlju ispod mojih nogu. Pločnik se zatalasao kao ocean, podižući djecu u plamen što proždire. I potres koji ih je digao u zrak kao *andjele* bez tezine, razdirući im majice u dronjke što su bičevali iza njih kao patrljci krila.

Šest tanušnih tijela se poput lepeze raširilo u područji eksplozije. Tamo gdje je bilo toliko pokreta i energije, sada je bila samo smrt. Čekao sam tjeskobno, užasnut, zastrašen. Napravio sam grimasu kad sam shvatio kao mi obično izgleda ova tragedija. Možda sam se prilagodio svom svijetu, naposlijetku.

Čekao sam da vidim sudbinu djece. Ukoliko su posjedovali tajnu, onda bi je možda neko od njih prenio u moj svijet. Ali niko od njih se nije pokrenuo. Iznenada, četvoro od njih su transcendirali.

Peto dijete je započelo groteskno putovanje kroz moju zemlju sjenki. Piljio sam u razmcvareno tijelo i buljio u oči, hladne i tamne kao jutarnji pepeo ponoćne lomače. Nije me mogao vidjeti, pošto je bio slijep, ali je osjećao moje prisustvo. Tvrdoglavo se grabio, bacakajući rukom kao novorodjenče koje se bori za prve udisaje zraka.

Uzeo sam mu ruku. Njegova ruka je bila sićušna i još uvijek topla, sa posljednjim tragovima života. Ili je to bila toplina eksplozije bombe. Dok sam ga vukao da ga oslobodim od njegovih upletenih preostataka, preko ponora izmedju svjetova, pogledao sam na gore i vidio šesto dijete, djevojčicu koja je bila predvodnik, kako me posmatra.

Nastavio sam da vučem, moju prvu brigu, dječaka ali bio sam zbunjen - djevojčica koje je zurila u mene nije nosila plazmičnu košuljicu. Krv je projurila njenim licem i njene krupne oči su zatreptale. Podsvjesno je brisala suze i pijesak iz očiju dok je gledala u mene sa dubokoumnošću što je bila jednaka mojoj.

Among them, I suddenly felt as invisible as I truly was. Even if I were not separated from them by death, they would not have seen me with their eyes glazed and transfixed by the spinning white ball. Their bodies coiled and sprang, and their limbs fluttered madly as they *danced* wildly in pursuit and expectation of the ball. For them, and for the moment, there was no other world.

But as it has now for months, the world invaded their fantasy. As the ball bounced up and away from the head of a small, energetic girl, a shadow passed like a lightning flash behind it.

No storm of nature could unleash a force like the bomb that drove into the earth under my feet. The pavement rippled like an ocean, lifting the children into a gout of flame and concussion that blew them like weightless *angels*, tattered T-shirts whipping behind them like the stumps of wings.

Six tiny bodies fanned out at the periphery of the blast radius. Where there had been so much motion and energy there was now only death. I waited anxiously, dreadfully. I grimaced as I realized how ordinary this tragedy seemed to me. Perhaps I had adapted to my world after all.

I waited to see the fate of the children. If they did possess a secret, then perhaps one of them would bring it to my world. But none of them moved. Then suddenly, four transcended.

A fifth began the grotesque journey to my land of shadows. I gazed at the torn body and stared into eyes as cold and dark as the morning ashes of a midnight bonfire. He couldn't see me, blinded as he was, but he sensed my presence. He grasped willfully with a thrashing hand as a newborn baby gasps that first breath of air.

I took it. His hand was tiny and still warm with the remnants of life. Or the heat of the bomb blast. As I pulled him free of his entangling remains and across the gulf between the worlds, I looked up to see the sixth, the young girl whose header had been so clean, watching me.

I continued reflexively to pull my first charge, the boy, but I was confused — the girl who stared at me wore no caul. Blood streaked her face, and her large eyes blinked. She subconsciously wiped tears and grit out of her eyes as she stared at me with a profundity equal to my own.

Sveti Vito Pleše za Vječnost

Shvatio sam da je bila živa. Nasmiješio sam joj se dok sam privijao dječaka na moje grudi i čvrsto sam prigrlio njegovo drhtureće tijelo. Uspjela je da mi uzvrati smiješkom. I klimnula je blago. Znala je. Bila je u šoku, i njen svijet je bio preokrenut naglavce ali ona je bila oslobodjena.

Sada je ona zaista posjedovala *tajnu* da je zaštiti od noćnih mora.

Zagrlio sam jače svoj oklop.

I realized that she was alive. I smiled at her as I lifted the boy to my chest where I closely hugged his shivering body. She managed to smile back. And she nodded slightly. Knowingly. She was in shock, and her world had been turned inside out, but she was relieved.

Now she truly possessed a *secret* to shield her from nightmares.

I hugged my own shield closer.

Author's Last Words

"Don't write any more books about us, you bastard. Give us back the guns the UN took from us."
Srebrenican woman after the July 1995 fall of her city as quoted in "Letter From Bosnia: We Hate You" (by David Rieff, *The New Yorker*, **Sept. 4, 1995)**

I was awfully young when I first encountered Bulwer-Lytton's eternal and eternally-used proverb "The pen is mightier than the sword." I don't believe I'd yet come to the conclusion that I wanted to be a writer (my first complete short story was a couple of years away), but the fact that I remember the details of my encounter with this jewel of the enlightened world has always said something to me in hindsight. It was a dynamic moment — the proverb said something I'd never considered, but I instantly and intuitively understood it and knew it to be true. There, very simply stated, is the greatest argument for writing.

The idea of changing the world by an act of personal will has been at the heart of both of my most ambitious writing projects. The first, a roleplaying game I wrote in 1993, held this tenet as its central theme. The second, the story you've just read, relies on this idea not as the theme of writing, but as the motive for writing it at all. In Bosnia I encountered a wrong so enormous that in lieu of swordplay, which the Untied Nations wasn't allowing anyway, I had to brandish my pen.

The first incarnation of this story ("Okay City One Thousand Times" in *Dark Destiny: Proprietors of Fate* edited by Edward E. Kramer) was a much less crafted work that was largely spawned by my outrage at the dichotomy of the reaction in the United States to the tragedies in Bosnia and the destruction of the bombing in Oklahoma City. I was stunned when I heard about the Federal Building blast on NPR. I imagined myself to be one of the parents of the children who died in that explosion. The unthinking assumption of safety I would have made when I left my child in the day-care service. The gut-wrenching shock at the attack that would take him or her away.

But later, I went numb when I extrapolated that explosion to Sarajevo, which I had been considering as the setting for a ghost story. The difference between the isolated event at the Federal Building and living in a world that had been just as normal as pre-blast Oklahoma City — but was now turned completely upside down and all-around by such attacks daily — was staggering. In Sarajevo, it wasn't only an unknown enemy who has come to hurt you. It wasn't only one building, perhaps your workplace, that was destroyed. It wasn't only losing your children or your wife or your husband. In Sarajevo it was neighbors, people you'd known for years, trying to destroy you. It was everything that formed your life — your mosque, your work, your home — being shelled. It was losing everyone you cared for, and having to deal daily with not just their sudden death, but the terrible and constant threat of their death.

It was one thousand times the toll in human lives. At least.

But, of course, Bosnia was half a world away. It wasn't in the heart of your very own nation. It would be ludicrous to expect the same kind of reaction. But that's why I took up my pen. Because the reaction should be the same.

No, the people in Bosnia aren't paying taxes to build our roads and send our children to school. And, no, they don't hold all the same beliefs that we do. But they are people just as innocent, just as deserving of safety, as anyone else. And for someone living in Maine or Alaska or Hawaii (or Germany or Japan or wherever, because allusions can be made to these places too if we draw on places like Kobe), is a person is Bosnia any more nameless than someone in the middle of the United States?

I can completely understand, though, if this sermonizing, if the message of the story, doesn't crack your lack of commitment. When I started that ghost story for that anthology about this time last year, I wasn't expecting to be moved either. That I was

Sveti Vito Pleše za Vječnost

moved is the power of that mighty pen, because as I wrote my story, I found that I never felt I quite knew enough about the Bosnians and their history. Every bit I learned made these people more familiar to me, and deepened my shock at their circumstances.

Eventually, though, I began to doubt. More than any physics or mathematics could hope to do, the war in Bosnia has convinced me that time is a malleable dimension. It definitely folds over on itself, because there are too many incidents that seem to have parallels through the ages, like an ink blot soaking through a folded sheet of paper.

As I wrote this story, I kept hoping that it would become outdated. I hoped the disaster would end, peace would ensue, and there would be less reason to finger-point and draw people's attention to the former Yugoslavia. Now that we've moved the Berlin Wall a few latitudes east, it would seem we could rest again. But that's silly. Just as silly as thinking that this book could ever be outdated. Just change the names, the year, the body count.

People don't learn from history. Moreover, how can we hope to stop the tide of history, how can it not repeat itself, when people obviously plot to perpetuate it? June 28, 1389/1914/1989. People can too easily ambush the future with the past. Just load a day — and it's probably possible with almost any day — with enough metaphor, and lo there comes more strife. Another genocide.

I reasoned that people just couldn't be moved. If several million deaths fifty years ago don't serve notice, then several thousand copies of this book now certainly won't either. What was the point in laboring so long over 15,000 words? I'm a bleeding heart with too much time on my hands — time enough to read so many books about Bosnia. Maybe I should heed the Srebrenican woman. What the Bosnians really need aren't more words, but more weapons. Maybe all my time should have been spent smuggling guns and ammunition to the soldiers.

But no matter how shaken my belief in the goodness of men and women, I cannot give up my belief in the pen. My mission, then, is in 15,000 words to distill the essence of all my reading, all the history of Bosnia, and all the tragedy of the present. It is words, after all, that began the bloody Balkan war — Slobodan Milosevic used words on one of those June 28ths to ambush history and bend it to his will and so bend the will of ethnic Serbians. No words can change what has happened, but every revolution starts with one. If this story can be that one for even one other, if it can be the fulcrum on which some event some one hundred decisions from now tilts, then it reaffirms the might of the pen.

Stewart von Allmen
April 1996

AFTERWORD: LEAVING YUGOSLAVIA

Michael Moorcock

It was raining as Jerry picked his way over the Belgrade bombsites followed by crowds of crippled children and the soft, pleading voices of the eleven- and twelve-year-old prostitutes of both sexes.

His clothes were stained and faded. Behind him were the remains of the crashed Sikorsky which had run out of fuel.

On foot he made for Dubrovnik, through a world ruled by bad poets who spoke the rhetoric of tabloid apocrypha and schemed for the fruition of a dozen seedy apocalypses.

At Dubrovnik the corpse-boats were being loaded up. Fuel for the automated factories of Anuradhapura and Angkor Wat. On one of them, if he was lucky, he might obtain a passage East.

Meanwhile machines grew skeletons and were fed with blood and men adopted metal limbs and plastic organs. A synthesis he found unwelcome.
**From *Sea Wolves*,
A Jerry Cornelius Story,
1969.**

SOMETIMES YOU REALLY wish you'd been wrong.

When, around the mid-sixties, I began to use Yugoslavia as a metaphor for all the potential conflicts bubbling under the surface of the Communist world — conflicts which had only been exacerbated by totalitarianism' — I was, like most visionary writers, trying to warn my readers of avoidable disaster. You write down the vision because perhaps superstitiously you think that if you say it, and make it fiction, maybe it won't happen. It is not the kind of successful prediction from which one draws any kind of satisfaction.

I anticipated war amongst the various unreconciled elements of the Communist empire because it was fairly clear that (as with the break up of the British Empire) war too frequently follows the collapse of imperial authority. So far, in fact, we have been singularly lucky that most of the territories gained or regained after the two world wars peacefully asserted their independence and sensibly recognised their interdependence. It is a tribute to those countries, where the black economy is now often the dominant economy, that they have so many sane politicians still in power.

I happen to believe that direct or indirect imperialism (whether British, U.S. Russian or Chinese) — the notion that one power somehow has a right or duty to control lesser powers — is the chief element in the creation of aggressive nationalism. Nationalism is usually a crude reaction to a threat, sometimes the actuality, of one's destiny being taken out of one's own hands.

Nationalism — disguised as patriotism — was the only alternative ideal ever allowed in former Communist countries, largely because it had little coherent political dialectic and could easily be coralled into the service of the authoritarian government.

Since I began travelling in the 1950s it has been evident to me that if ever the European Communist Empire (referred to ironically as the new Byzantine Empire by many of its citizens) collapsed, it would result in a dramatic descent into quasi-fascistic nationalism and, unless this was carefully anticipated and dealt with, that inevitably meant bloody warfare somewhere and probably some form of genocide. Racism, virtually unchanged from its 19th century forms, is for instance endemic to Eastern Europe, in a way that is shocking to most modern Western Europeans. Czechs, often proud of what they call their 'philoSemiticism', can be vicious on the subject of gypsies, for instance, and many Poles are by no means upset about the Holocaust.

In the absence of evident social justice, people turn to less efficient means than democratic secularism to provide themselves with a sense of order and self-worth. The emphasis on ethnicity in the US, which began from the best of motives in the late sixties and produced dozens of books and movies about 'being Jewish' or 'being Italian' or 'being African', while intending to encourage people's self-esteem by emphasising their cultural history (as well as all too frequently established stereotypes of themselves), actually helped in the disintegration of the US into the country of antagonistic tribes it now threatens to become. In the absence of moral rigor in those who can most readily afford to cultivate it at the top, those at the bottom see no reason to behave any differently than their supposed exemplars. As in certain Middle Eastern states, the lie has today become a common instrument of social intercourse.

...

If the Croats were part of the Reich, we'd have them serving as faithful auxiliaries of the German Fuehrer, to police our marshes. Whatever happens, one shouldn't treat them as Italy is doing at present. The Croats are a proud people. They should be bound directly to the Fuehrer by an oath of loyalty. Like that, one could rely upon them absolutely. When I have Kvaternik standing in front of me, I behold the very type of the Croat as I've always known him, unshakeable in his friendships, a man whose oath is eternally binding. The Croats are very keen on not being regarded as Slavs. According to them,

they're descended from the Goths. The fact that they speak a Slav language is only an accident, they say.
**ADOLF HITLER,
29th October 1941,
Private Conversation,
Hitler's Table Talk.**

...

Most of the attempts we make at social engineering, whether socialist, monetarist (the current favourite) or totalitarian, conservative or liberal, seem to result in a greater mess in the end. In the absence of justice promised by the Left, says Andrea Dworkin, people look for order from the Right. As in Weimar and early 20th century Italy, both of which had near-perfect democratic constitutions, they follow demagogues. They often vote demagogues, whose rhetoric is pretty much always the same as, say, Pat Buchanan's, to supreme power, and then regret it, as happened in Italy and Germany, the Iberian Peninsula and much of the Balkans between the two world wars.

The demagogues always speak to the middle-class of their insecurities and remind working people of their historical rights, their earlier greatness, their 'alien' enemies who are taking their jobs, stealing their money. Those same demagogues always wind up favouring the powerful, courting Big Business (which usually has a large hand in the malaise) and privately acting to reassure it that all the populist rhetoric is really no more than a means to power.

Power is what these people want, above all, and at any price, including your life and mine. By voting for simplified notions and simplistic slogans, we inevitably vote for our own destruction. In both Italy and Germany in the 20s and 30s the people who voted Mussolini and Hitler to power soon found their real incomes shrinking dramatically — authoritarianism, always favoured by conservatives, international corporations and communists alike, since it is a system which silences all those irritating disagreeing voices, runs a *very* inefficient economy. There always comes a time when it really needs a good war as a distraction and an economic boost...

The Yugoslav versions of that typically authoritarian rhetoric are even more simple, of course, since complexity is anathema to fascists and communists alike, and simple sound-bite explanations of complex events keep a population ignorant and controllable. As in our inner cities, where an alternative economy and story is up and running, this situation always leads to 'secret' popular histories running parallel (like the black market or the drug market) to the official versions, and offering a tribal story told in terms of folk heroes and racial superiority, in contrast to the media's official version.

The dream of Greater Serbia has been with us, in one form or another, for the better part of one and a half millennia, although it did not really take a modern form until the rise of the famous Black Hand — the *Cerna Ruka* — a nationalist army group officially known as *Ujedinjenje ili Smrt* (Unity or Death) led by Dragutin Dimitrievitch which worked in unison with the Serbian Prime Minister Nichola Pasitch, whom many believe to be the real father of what became Yugoslavia. The Black Hand feared the imperialist ambitions of Austria-Hungary, especially after the Austrian annexation of Bosnia-Herzogovenia.

The Black Hand, which committed political assassinations as a casual policy, was born of a specific murder, the successful plot to kill the Serbian King Alexander Obrenovitch in 1903. Fearing the likelihood of Serbia being divided by the creation of a South-Slav State consisting of Slovenia, Croatia, Bosnia, Herzegovina and Dalmatia, which would have mollified much of their broad support, they planned their most historically significant murder, the assassination of the Archduke Francis Ferdinand in Sarejevo in 1914, which led directly to the beginning of the First World War, the Bolshevik Revolution, the Italian and German totalitarian states, the Holocaust, the Second World War and the dropping of the atomic bomb on Hiroshima, which in turn had enormous consequences from which we all still suffer on a daily basis. Not bad for an obscure bunch of nationalist conservatives in a small Balkan State most people couldn't easily find on the map and whose names are pretty thoroughly forgotten.

When the Yugoslav State was formed after the First World War (in the hope, among other things, of creating a nation large enough to resist potential aggression from countries like Italy and Germany, which still fostered very real imperial ambitions in the Balkan Peninsula), the six countries which made up Yugoslavia all had long, important histories. Between them, in recent centuries, they had fought Turks, Austrians, Hungarians and Italians as well as one another.

At different times over the centuries, Slovenia, Croatia, Bosnia-Herzogovina, Serbia, Montenegro and Macedonia had beaten back dozens of aggressors, had flourished as independent states and peoples and had also been vanquished by virtually all the conquerors who swept back and forth across Europe since before the time of Christ. Legitimately, these countries developed powerful mythologies, folk heroes, legends of former glory which spoke of times when they had brought enlightenment, or terror or religion to their region.

In the mythologies, for instance, of Serbia, legends abound of both natural and supernatural enemies (generally from the East) driven off by valiant warrior-princes. The Serbs can look back to a history rich with exemplary heroes who arose at times of crisis to fight against some rival, who challenged the Byzantine Empire and even came close to conquering it on more than one occasion. Westerners have only a dim notion of the profound imaginative power which Byzantium still holds in the region. Here is where Greek Orthodox Byzantium and Ottoman Islam frequently clashed (and sometimes united) and left their stamp on everything.

Of course, those rivals of the Serbs were often enemies who believed themselves short-changed in some temporary alliance, or wanted more land, or revenge or felt that Serbia threatened their power in some way. They could always get enough people together to die for their ambitions by reminding those serfs, vassals, clans and burghers of how cruel and bloodthirsty the Serbs (or Bulgars or Romanians or Hungarians or Macedonians or Slovenians or Albanians) had been last time and how it was up to them to do exactly the same thing back (and thus keep the entire bloody game running for centuries) and, moreover, extend the might of Greater Serbia, Romania, Hungary, Albania etc. over the less enlightened and crueler peoples of the region...

"I have a great, an almost gigantic task. I am called to weld together the two great South-Slav peoples, the Serbs and Croats, into one national unit. I fully realize that this task is as enormous as it is dangerous. But nothing can deter me from completing my mission."
**Alexander Karageorgevitch,
Second King of the Serbs, Croats and Slovenes, and first King of Yugoslavia in 1926,
ten years before he was assassinated.**

As Stewart von Allmen's thoughtful parable suggests, imperialism, whether it be Napoleon's, the United States' expansion into Indian territories, British expansion into Africa, or the Soviet Union's and China's ferocious suppression of neighbouring states, always has to be explained to the foot soldiers and cannon fodder in some idealistic way. Suckers that we are, we are therefore almost always being sent to save some poor benighted aliens from the error of their ways (Zulus, Sioux, Vietnamese), whether they like it or not, and wondering why they are so damned ungrateful. Even on the most amiable level it leads at very least to resentments, such as the highly-publicised building in Bosnia of an expensive bridge by the US military that could have been done far more easily, cheaply and efficiently if the Americans had actually listened to the locals.

Therefore, it is never surprising when, as a people, our good intentions and well-meaning sentiments are perceived as an imperial threat by other peoples who are well aware of our own histories, get our TV programmes by satellite, and are all-too-familiar with the lies our politicians still tell us, and which we still believe, in order to make us go to war and die undignified, violent and pointless deaths.

Quite reasonably, those other peoples frequently don't see a lot of difference between us, the well-meaning democrats, and them, the bloody-handed expansionist warlords — because in the end, in terms of actual effect, there *is* very little difference. We may perceive certain differences of intention and meaning in our actions, but the degrees are often very fine, predominantly those of scale, or proximity or of perspective. The difference, if you like, between slaughtering a cow yourself and buying a piece of it wrapped in sterile plastic in a supermarket. Whether you admit it to yourself or not, you know really that someone, somewhere, has to do that killing for you.

The result of our passive acceptance of our nations' imperialism, however, is very similar and has many of the characteristics of genocide. whether we are destroying defeated, fleeing soldiers and civilians on the Basra Road or supporting bloody-handed expansionist regimes in our own national self-interest (as with Nigeria or Indonesia, for instance — and as we had earlier done with South Africa and Iraq) we have the same *effect* on the innocent woman or child maimed and dying and probably raped in the ruins of their home.

Because we accept the truth as CNN tells it, we are not very far away from being that despicable, wolfish-looking Serb or Croat, that unshaven fashion-victim, clutching some hideously lethal toy and wading through the filthy wasteland he has made of his own back yard.

While we good-hearted democrats continue to enjoy the wealth we take for granted as a result of our own nations' involvement with or passive support of violence at home and abroad, we are morally very little different to that violent brute. In his circumstances, we might easily be him — or worse, her. As a people, with our constitutional power, we are actually able to tell our governments to stop. We are able to tell our governments to behave better in our name. We are able to tell them to negotiate and not to fight, to feed and not to starve, to make friends, not enemies. Yet only rarely do we appear to want to do it.

In the polling booths, we seem to prefer appeals to our immediate greed and childish insecurities usually instilled in us by the politicians we are then asked to vote for. However, that is no reason to dismiss the notion of elected government. If we want a better world, it is up to us to tell those elected representatives what to do and how to behave. There's a very simple, basic, democratic principle involved here — Their power should come from nothing but our votes. If it does not, then it is not legitimate power.

If it comes from private capital or foreign governments, that power is not legitimate power. And there, ironically, is where my views, as a cosmopolitan and a strong supporter of, for instance, a federated Europe, meet those of the nationalist. As much as possible in a harmonious society, we need to be able to steer our own course. What we need to be exploring more vigorously are ways of establishing the rule of commonly agreed laws to which every single human being can appeal without losing any direct control over their own lives. It would seem to be a fairly easy problem to solve...

It is somewhat difficult for a foreigner to realize the differences that exist between Serbs and Croats. The Allied statesmen, who during the war received the mass of propaganda in the interest of the creation of a new South-Slav State, must have been bewildered. Here were two nations akin to each other both in race and language, Serbs and Croats were branches of the Slavonic migration which left Northern Europe in the sixth century and settled in the sixth and seventh centuries in the territories which now constitute Yugoslavia. Thus there is the common cradle, the brotherly and neighbourly life after the immigration; and there is the almost common language. And yet both nations carefully preserve their own traditions, history, culture, and other peculiarities, and neither is willing to sacrifice these peculiarities to the idea of the creation of a homogeneous nation.

**M.V.Fodor,
Foreign correspondent for *The Manchester Guardian* and *The American Mercury*,
in *South of Hitler*, 1937.**

Any man's death diminishes me, for I am involved in mankind, wrote Donne. Any woman's rape diminishes me as a man because I am involved in mankind. Any society that believes rape to be justifiable — or, even worse, an instrument of policy — is a shameful and brutal society. And any society which diminishes the importance of the crime of rape or murder, is to some degree guilty of the rapes and murders which follow. Though we may control them to a degree, we do not stop such crimes occurring by sending international police forces to the scene (the crimes are, after all, occurring in almost as large numbers in our own countries where we have been spectacularly unsuccessful in stopping them happening) but by re-ordering our world, socially and economically, on a juster, saner and safer basis, by listening to other voices.

It does not take elaborate or simplistic political systems or creeds to establish such justice, sanity and safety in the world — but it does take a lot of negotiation, education, imagination and intelligence. It takes a lot of silence, of hard thinking. It takes a lot of understanding, of realisation of our increasing interdependency as a race. It takes a belief that a better future exists for us all, through mutual respect and working together, an acknowledgement of what the rich nations owe to the poor ones, of how we sometimes make them poor by virtue of our wealth, of how we may all work towards creating a fairer and less violent world. And most of all it takes a genuine and positive will to good, irrespective of one's political temperament.

These were the simple ideals of the people who put the first United Nations charter together after the Second World War. The Cold War was a major hindrance to that dream of world harmony and its consequences remain with us, but because the United Nations (underfunded as it is — and owed billions by the U.S. alone) has failed to stop violence does not mean that the United Nations is a failure. We need, however, to work out ways of using the U.N. machinery a lot better than we're using it at the moment and making sure it has real power (which means real money and real commitment, as well as real vigilance as to how that money is spent). To use it again, as George Bush did in the Gulf operation, as an umbrella for the ambitions of the U.S. and her allies, would make it nothing more than an instrument of imperialism and lose it all value as a means of achieving reconciliation and peace.

An important part of von Allmen's message is that while we should not trust leaders, we *should* trust our own instincts to good. If leaders do not help us make those instincts manifest, but instead pervert them in order to fulfill less noble ambitions, we, the electorate, should hold them to account. And we should seek ways of putting those feelings into action through our own will to peace — for until our will to peace is as aggressive as our will to war, not a single one of us in the world today shall ever be free of the threat of suffering a brutal, bloody and unjust death, whether it be in Sarajevo, Belfast, Tel Aviv or Oklahoma City.

It is not easy to find ways of putting such principles into action. However, I believe it to be a matter of urgency, probably of survival, that we start finding ways and means pretty quickly, before it's too late for all of us. I come from a generation which found a common idealism in the Blitz, which discovered in itself a courage and self-respect no politician had ever believed existed! I know from that experience that ordinary people have a positive instinct towards the best they can be. The same thing has been observed in Sarajevo. Perhaps we should feel ashamed that it takes something as foul as war to harness that kind of courage and then employ it in such wasteful and pointless ways.

But there's always hope, because there are always people willing to make that extra effort in the cause of sanity and social harmony.

Stories like *Saint Vitus Dances Eternity* help in that effort as do the circumstances of its publication. In the form of an entertaining supernatural tale, von Allmen has made a universal and important observation. It is what the best kind of popular fiction does. It has been a privilege to write this afterword.

**Michael Moorcock,
Lost Pines, Texas
March 1996**

[1] **Which Americans continue to confuse with socialism so that they're capable of forming the notion of 'corporate socialism', by which they seem to mean the totalitarian rule of Big Business, something very close to fascism or national socialism.**

BIBLIOGRAPHY

Some selected titles that I found extremely useful when researching details and history for this story.

Dizdarević, Zlatko,
Sarajevo: A War Journal,
Henry Holt and Company 1993.

The author wrote this series of columns while he remained as an editor at Oslobodenje, the Sarajevo daily newspaper mentioned in my story. More than any other I read, it was this book that made me aware of the tragedy that was occurring in Bosnia.

Drakulić, Slavenka,
The Balkan Express,
HarperCollins 1993.

This book was written by a woman who lives in Zagreb and who possesses both an insider's perspective and an outsider's view.

Filipović, Zlata,
Zlata's Diary,
Viking 1994.

The Anne Frank of Sarajevo — this young girl's diary shows how her world came apart. Very easy reading that puts the events in perspective.

Gutman, Roy,
A Witness to Genocide,
Macmillan 1993.

From the Pulitzer Prize-winning *Newsday* correspondent, this book is one a number of books from foreign journalists. This is definitely one of the best of that group.

Karahasan, Dzevad,
Sarajevo, Exodus of a City,
Kodansha International 1994.

I read no better portrait of this awesome city. To truly understand the cultural legacy that this war destroyed, read this book. There is an incredible Afterword from Slavenka Drakulić that brings up the issue I touch on in my Last Words herein.

Malcolm, Noel,
Bosnia: A Short History,
New York University Press 1994.

An extraordinary book that provides a comprehensive view of the people of the Balkans for the last two thousand years. The book is especially useful for those whose familiarity with the region does not extend much beyond the June 28, 1914 assassination of the Archduke Franz Ferdinand.

Vulliamy, Ed,
Seasons in Hell,
St. Martin's Press 1994.

Another journalist's account of the war, but this one has a very stirring mix of detail and overview.

BIOGRAPHIES

Stewart von Allmen

Aida Mušanović

Michael Moorcock

Born in Illinois in 1968, Stewart has always pursued a career in writing and publishing. His first professional publication came in 1985, and in 1986 he helped form a publishing company. His writing has consistently grown from its genre roots — though his first novel (CONSPICUOUS CONSUMPTION, Harper Prism, June 1995) was a genre horror book — and his company has grown from the producer of a domestic game-related magazine to a prominent international publisher of novels and games based near Atlanta, Georgia.

The novelette SAINT VITUS DANCES ETERNITY: A SARAJEVO GHOST STORY is Stewart von Allmen's second book. A number of his short stories have appeared in various anthologies, and he is currently writing a multi-volume work of fiction set in the near future.

Thank you so much—
  Aida
  Chris
  Gretchen
  Larry
  Michael

Your contributions to this work are deeply appreciated.

Aida Mušanović lived the life of a refugee in Croatia, Germany and Holland after her escape from Sarajevo during the first winter of the war in Bosnia in 1992. It was after her flight from her homeland — and while in Holland in particular — that she became involved in a series of public activities to raise awareness of the genocidal aggression that has been taking place in Bosnia. In particular, she was connected with several women's groups and also served as the Bosnian spokeswoman at the annual United Nations of Youth conference in the Hague.

Aida now resides in the United States, and it is since her arrival there that she helped organize the international show "Sarajevo Expo '92," an art exhibition that toured in Australia, most of the major cities in Europe, and in several U.S. cities: Seattle, Portland, Haverford, Washington, D.C. and New York City. The exhibition consisted of the work of eighteen Bosnian artists, among whom Aida was the youngest, that portrayed their individual and collective reactions to the horrors of the Bosnian war.

Of this book, Aida said: "I feel very proud to have the opportunity to create the art for SAINT VITUS DANCES ETERNITY. My art is an homage to all the Bosnian citizens — Croats, Jews, Muslims, Serbs and others — who have fought or who have died fighting for the right to live in an undivided, secular, democratic, multi-ethnic Bosnia."

To My Dear:
  Alma Mušanović, Betty Winkler, Inge Pompen, Matko Zelić and Nadira Sijerčić.
  —thank you for your love and support.

The artwork originals were printed at:
  Yama Prints
  140 West 30th Street, 4th Floor
  New York, NY 10001

Now a resident of the United States, Michael Moorcock was born in London in 1939 and published hi first novel in 1962. From 1964 to 1980 he edited the seminal imaginative fiction magazine New Worlds, where her remains consulting editor. Moorcock has written more than eighty works of fiction and non-fiction. The Condition of Muzak won the Guardian Fiction Prize, and Mother London was shortlisted for the Whitbread Prize. He has also written and performed with the rock groupss Blue Oyster Cult and Hawkwind.

He has won the World Fantasy Award, the Nebula Award, the August Derleth Award and the British Fantasy Award.

Sveti Vito Pleše za Vječnost